OPERATION FOX HUNT

Survival or slaughter...

Field-Marshal Eugen von Schwartau, the Caucasian Fox, led his Nazi stormtroopers to the very gates of Moscow, striking terror into the heartland of Russia. Now, with the fortunes of war temporarily going against the Germans, von Schwartau had his troops poised for a crippling attack on the Russian oilfields. The Allies needed commandos that could be as cunning and as deadly as the Caucasian Fox himself. The Destroyers, led by the wild, one-eyed Mark Crooke, were the only men who could meet terror with terror, and their orders included the death of the Caucasian Fox himself.

OPERATION FOX HUNT

OPERATION FOX HUNT

by

Charles Whiting

Magna Large Print Books
Long Preston, North Yorkshire,
BD23 4ND, England.

British Library Cataloguing i

Whiting, Charles
    Operation fox hunt.

    A catalogue record of
    available from the Bri

    ISBN   0-7505-2374-3

Published in Large Print 2005 by arrangement with
Eskdale Publishing

Magna Large Print is an imprint of Library Magna Books Ltd.

Printed and bound in Great Britain by
T.J. (International) Ltd., Cornwall, PL28 8RW

SECTION ONE:
THE PLAN

'The Fox must die – and die soon!'
Admiral Godfrey, Director of Naval
Intelligence to Destroyers
May 1943

CHAPTER ONE

Abruptly the thick smoke of battle was pierced by the bulk of a charging tank. It was a T-34. The watchers recognised it at once. They could clearly see the red Soviet star on its turret. It braked to a halt in a cloud of dust. For a moment it remained, its long overhanging 76mm cannon swinging round like the snout of some primeval monster searching for its prey. At the anti-tank gun near the burning farmhouse, the survivors were still paralysed by the T-34's first shell which had shattered the right side of the armoured shield. The wounded loader sat awkwardly on the ground staring at the stump which had once been his leg, the blood running unchecked from the wound. The layer, unhurt but obviously shocked, stared as if mesmerised at the Russian tank which must spot them at any moment. Behind him the Obergefreiter sprawled over the metal trail – dead.

Clods of earth shot up as the T-34 lurched forward again. It had seen the Germans. Its machine gun began to chatter. A stream of tracer stitched the air. The Russians were making the Germans keep their heads down. The watchers, who had all been through the same experience themselves at one time or another in these last terrible years, knew the tactic all too well.

The T-34 grew steadily closer. One hundred and fifty yards, one hundred, seventy-five. By the gun, the Germans remained immobile. Even the tracer bouncing off the shield could not shake them out of their apathy. It was as if they had accepted their fate, as if it had been ordained by some god of war that they must die on this nameless Russian battlefield in the next few seconds.

At fifty yards the T-34 lurched to a halt. The watchers could see every detail now – the bedrolls, the spare lengths of track, the helmets, even the Russian cooking pots hanging from the turret.

Suddenly a tall figure in grey Wehrmacht uniform, devoid of any badges of rank, was sprinting across the rutted field, rifle in hand, the tails of his ankle-length greatcoat flapping against his muddy jackboots. The tank gunner spotted him. Lead stitched the air. Dust spurted up around his feet. But the

German seemed to bear a charmed life. Zigzagging crazily through the shell-holes, he avoided the Russian bullets.

Skidding to a stop like an American baseball player, he threw down his rifle. With a kick he pushed the dead man off the trail, elbowed the mesmerised layer aside and crouched down behind the gun. He shouted something. His back was to the watchers, but they could see his words had an effect. The layer grabbed a shell from the clip on the shield, yanked back the breech and rammed home the shell.

The next instant the tall man fired. He had had no time to sight the gun. He simply pulled the firing lever. The anti-tank gun shuddered. The breech rumbled back and for a moment the smoke in front of the muzzle obscured the watchers' view. When it cleared it revealed a gaping hole in the turret of the T-34. One track was flapping behind it and the dead driver was sprawled half out of the lower escape hatch, little tongues of flame already beginning to lick at his body.

For a second, the Germans at the gun did not move. Then they threw up their hands in triumph, as the tank began to blaze. Suddenly all was elation. Half-a-dozen high-ranking officers appeared as if from nowhere, their fat chests covered with decorations, their heavy faces sparkling with joy. They pumped the tall soldier's hand and slapped him on the back excitedly. The watchers got a last glimpse of him in close-up – broad, good-humoured face with clever eyes and high Slavonic cheekbones. Then the screen went blank. The watchers became aware of the whirring projector which reminded them that the battle they had just witnessed had taken place over three thousand miles away.

Commander Miles Mallory of Naval Intelligence switched off the projector. He walked over to the tall French windows of Room 38, the office of his chief, Admiral Godfrey, and pulled back the heavy blackout curtains. Outside it was raining. Mallory stared at the fat slug of a barrage balloon which seemed to hang directly above Number Ten Downing Street, as if Mr Churchill had ordered it for his own personal protection against the hit-and-run raiders who were presently plaguing London. He took out one of his expensive hand-rolled cigarettes. Fitting it into his elegant ivory holder, he lit it and turned to the men staring at him expectantly. 'I suppose

14

you are wondering what that was all about?'

'Sure,' the tall yellow-faced Texan with the improbable name of Lone Star Alamo Jones drawled cynically. 'And when do we get to see the Mickey Mouse?' He looked at the immaculately uniformed naval officer with ill-concealed contempt.

Mallory did not like the American, whom his colleagues – without much originality – called the Yank. But he valued his killing ability. He promised himself that when the time was ripe he'd get him posted to somewhere suitably exotic – like the Outer Hebrides.

'I'm afraid you don't get to see it, Jones. We thought it might be beyond your intellectual capacity.'

Stevens, the cunning little cockney who had masqueraded as a colonel in the Western Desert, running his own thriving black market organisation with two hundred fellow deserters before the MPs finally picked him up, nudged Jones in the ribs. 'He got yer that time.'

'That's enough.' Crooke, VC, the one-eyed leader of this band of thugs who styled themselves 'The Detroyers,' asserted his authority. 'Let Commander Mallory get on with it.'

'Thank you, Crooke. Well,' Mallory began, 'what you just saw was a captured German Army newsreel of last year's fighting in the Caucasus.' He nodded towards the German communist member of the gang, 'Courtesy of the Red Army, by the way. Thaelmann. We borrowed it from the Soviet Embassy in London. Had to go right up to the top to get it – to Ambassador Maisky himself.'

'Why?' Crooke asked.

'Because it's the only photographic material available on Field-Marshal Eugen von Schwartau, presently commander of the German 20th Caucasian Army. Apparently he's a soldier's soldier. He doesn't go in for publicity business like Rommel – or our own little seven-day wonder,' Mallory added somewhat maliciously.

'Can't say I've ever heard of him,' Stevens said.

'But you know his nickname well enough,' Mallory answered him. 'His men call him the Caucasian Fox.'

Their reaction was instantaneous. 'He's the chap who nearly took Moscow in 1941, when the Jerries first attacked Russia,' one of them said brightly.

'That's right Peters. That's the chap.'

The big ex-Guards sergeant-major, who

16

had been sent to the Cairo Military Prison for refusing to go into action, where he had remained in the company of his fellow Destroyers until Crook came along and fetched them all out for employment on special duties, stroked his chin thoughtfully. 'By all accounts, sir, he's one of the best the Jerries have got.'

'And you are showing us these movable pictures,' Gippo, the half-breed who claimed to be an illegitimate descendant of Lord Kitchener, said in his broken English, 'because you are wishing us to have something on him?'

'Yes, you brown rogue,' a hearty voice answered for Mallory. 'Got it in one.'

The Destroyers sprang to attention.

Admiral Godfrey, the head of Naval Intelligence, was standing at the door, wiping the raindrops off his face. He motioned them to sit down again and, taking off his coat, he said: 'Just got back from a watery lunch with the Joint Intelligence Chiefs.' He turned to Mallory. 'They've agreed, Miles. The op's on.'

'What op, sir?' Crooke asked.

'Operation Caucasian Fox. We want you and your bunch of tame thugs to go to Russia.'

17

'And then, sir?'

'Then? Oh, then,' he said as if it were the most natural thing in the world on this wet May afternoon in the heart of official London, 'we want you to kill him.'

He walked over to the old-fashioned wooden stand and hung up his coat. Almost conversationally, he said: 'Ruddy awful weather, isn't it?' His thumb came down on the brass bell which was the centrepiece of his desk. 'Now then, where's my tea?'

CHAPTER TWO

'Your tea, sir,' the pretty red-headed Wren came in with the cups rattling on the tray.

He smiled at her. 'You're new, aren't you?'

Mallory grinned, took in the girl's attractive figure and thought to himself that the Admiral, who always maintained he liked 'all my girls to be well-bred and have good legs,' obviously hadn't lost his taste for a pretty face.

'Yes sir,' the girl said, a little embarrassed, as she passed out the cups. 'I've just been posted to the DNI from the Belgian section.'

'I see,' Godfrey said, taking in the 'BELGIQUE' patch on her navy blue tunic.

'How would you like it?' she asked Peters, bending over to offer him the sugar and exposing a few more inches of obviously non-Government-issue black silk stockings.

Gippo winked at Stevens and whispered. 'I know how I am liking it.'

Stevens looked at him in mock horror. 'That's typical wog for you. That's all your

19

kind can think about!'

Finally the Wren was finished and Mallory continued his briefing. 'Let me tell you a little more about our reasons' – he nodded in the Admiral's direction – 'for calling you here today. I am sure you have all noticed that there is a campaign going on in this country at the moment to force the Prime Minister to launch the Second Front in Europe this year.'

Crooke put down his cup and touched the black patch which covered his empty eye socket, the result of his part in the abortive raid on Rommel's HQ that had won him the Victoria Cross and lost him his eye. 'You mean those scrawls you see in the underground and the like?' he asked.

'Yes, that's the sort of thing.'

'Communist organised,' Crooke snapped. 'Any fool can see that.'

Godfrey lowered his cup. 'You may be right, but none the less the PM is most anxious that we help our – er Russian allies.' He enunciated the words as if they were in italics. 'Naturally it's impossible for him to even think of a Second Front this year. In '44 perhaps, but certainly not this year.' He nodded to Mallory and grunted. 'Miles, you'd better explain. This whole business is getting far too complicated for my poor old brain.'

'Thank you, Admiral. Well, we know from a very delicate source that the Germans will soon attempt to make up for their defeat at Stalingrad by launching a major attack on the Russian front, probably in the next six weeks. We have already informed the Russian High Command – the Stavka – of the German plans and undoubtedly Moscow has taken appropriate counter-measures. Our guess is that the Russians will try to catch the Germans off-balance once they have launched their offensive and hit them in either their southern or northern flank. The PM thinks it will be below Stalingrad, where the Russians still have their best troops, probably in the Caucasus. Now–'

'Do you mean to say, sir,' Crooke suddenly interrupted, 'that we don't know the Russians' intentions? We compromise the greatest intelligence secret of the war – that we have broken the code of the German High Command – that "very delicate source," as you call it, by telling Stalin and he won't even tell us what his counter-measures are going to be!'

Mallory was not put out. He lit another of his expensive cigarettes and stuck it in his

21

holder. 'Pace, pace, Crooke! Hold your horses and let me explain,' he said calmly. 'We have transmitted the information to them without their knowing it came from us.'

'How?'

Mallory looked across at the Admiral, who gave a barely perceptible nod of assent. 'You remember the camp the boche put you into and the Red Orchestra men you met there – from the German branch of the Communist spy ring?' he asked.

'Yes, I remember them,' Steven said. 'I thought the Jerries had rounded them all up last year.'

'Not all, Stevens. There is another group operating on neutral territory – in Switzerland to be exact – under the leadership of an Hungarian publisher called Rado. I can't tell you much more but we have one of our agents working with the group – an apparently convinced Red. We used him to pass on the information about the forthcoming German attack. In short the Russkies don't know the info comes from us. They think it's from their own spies. As I was saying, we feel that the Russkies will try to turn the German flank in the Caucasus. For two reasons. It's Russia's most valued piece of real estate, because of the oilfields there. And Hitler has a thing about the place.'

'Why sir?' the Guardsman asked.

'Oil. He's obsessed by the stuff. For him it's progress – the modern world. Our people in Berlin tell us that he's read everything worth reading on the subject. And it was because of his initial drive into the area that Caucasian Fox got his promotion to Field-Marshal. As we interpret Russian thinking on the subject, the plan must go something like this. They know the Führer's obsession with Caucasus. Accordingly there are strong forces there, including some of the élite divisions of the German Army, Rommel's old 7th Armoured, for instance. As a result the German High Command won't expect an attack there. However, Stalin is an Oriental and that is just the place where he will attack.'

'I can see that, sir,' Stevens broke in. 'But where do we come in?'

Mallory smiled admiringly. 'You're the new post-war world, Stevens; you'll go far in civvy street.'

'I intend to, sir,' the cockney said modestly. 'If your lot let me get out of the Kate Karney alive.'

'So what is the role of the Destroyers? The Russkies expect us to back up their great counter-offensive with an attack through France. We can't! We haven't got the men or the equipment. But we can get rid of the great barrier in the way of Russkies' success in the Caucasus.'

'The Caucasian Fox?' Crooke asked grimly.

Mallory nodded. 'That's right.'

'Crikey,' Stevens groaned and clutched his forehead in mock anguish. 'This is more complicated than Edgar Wallace. How are we common folk supposed to follow all this, sir?'

'You aren't,' Mallory said cheerfully, noting that not a trace of fear had passed over the faces of his tame thugs at the mention of the new op. 'That's to be left to the officers and gentlemen.'

'It's the rich what has the pleasure and the poor what gets the blame,' Stevens commented.

'Perhaps,' Mallory answered. 'Now let's get on with the business.' He pointed at the back door of Number Ten, which could be seen through the window. 'It has been decided over there that our – your – contribution to the great offensive will be the elimination of the Caucasian Fox. Without him, the German front will collapse under the weight of the Russian attack. It is the PM's hope – and he's under a great deal of pressure from Stalin – that the Russians won't be too insistent on a Second Front if their offensive in the Caucasus succeeds.'

'Yes,' Admiral Godfrey broke in, 'Mr Churchill is emphatic on that point. Yesterday he told the Joint Intelligence Chiefs that we could not afford to engage in offensive operations in France if we are to carry out our commitments in the Med now we have seen the Hun off in Tunisia.' He cleared his throat and raised his voice, as if he were going to address the whole ship's company of one of the battle cruisers he had commanded before the war. 'I don't want to be melodramatic about this, but you *must* achieve your objective. Perhaps the whole course of future British operations will depend upon your eliminating the Caucasian Fox. The Fox must die – and die soon!'

He ran his eyes round their pale faces, sizing each one of them up, knowing the thoughts that must be running through their heads at this moment, as they realised what the new operation meant: one more step on the road to an appointment with violent death.

'But I don't quite understand, sir.' It was Thaelmann who broke the sudden silence. 'Why can't–'

'You don't have to, Thaelmann,' Mallory cut him short. 'We've been told that you're not going on this op.' And before the German could react, he turned to the American. 'Neither are you, Jones.'

The Yank half rose. 'In a pig's ass!' he burst out. 'What the hell is this!'

Crooke held up his hand to silence him. His face was white with anger.

'Why?' he demanded. 'Who said so?'

The Commander took a last puff at his cigarette, while the Admiral studied his empty cup, as if embarrassed. Mallory busied himself with the task of fitting another cigarette into his holder.

'I asked you a question,' Crooke said coldly.

'I know,' Mallory said quietly, 'and I'm going to give you an answer. Or rather I'm going to let the chap who is running this op for MI6 give you the gen. A chap called Philby. Mr Kim Philby.'

CHAPTER THREE

While he waited in the Athenaeum for Mr Philby, whose club this was, Crooke glanced idly at the *Daily Express*. He didn't like the paper particularly, but he knew its owner Lord Beaverbrook, who had been instrumental in getting him his Victoria Cross the year before, believed in the future of the British Empire as passionately as he did himself. The front page with its banner headline 'The Avalanche Surrender' was full of the German surrender in Tunisia. Idly he glanced at the column entitled 'Invasion May Start in a Week' and read 'The Berlin Warning.'

'Invasion warnings were sounded to the German and Italian people in "keep calm" radio calls last night. Berlin pointed out that no long respite could be expected while the Allies regrouped, and added that "one week at the most will elapse before the Allied armies have their full fighting power." ... "An Allied invasion could be made across the North Sea, the Channel or on a southern front," said General Bollati on Rome radio.' Crooke stared at the central photo, showing a group of Italian POWs in the desert above the caption 'Laughing their way to the prison camp.' To him the article seemed another example of the pressure being put on the British Government to invade France. As far as he could judge there was no sign of an invasion army being readied in Britain for the cross-Channel venture. The dry, apparently objective article was yet another part of the underground campaign being waged by the British Communist Party to force the country into immediate action.

'Good evening, Lieutenant C-C-Crooke?' a soft voice, impaired by a bad stammer, enquired.

Crooke looked up.

A medium-sized man of his own age in a shabby tweed jacket and baggy grey flannels was staring down at him, a friendly grin on his mild face. He rose to his feet. 'Yes, that's right.' The newcomer stuck out his hand. 'Let me introduce myself. Harold Adrian Russell Philby – people call me Kim. You can if you like.'

They shook hands, but Crooke ignored the offer made by the shabby civilian. He was too angry at him. 'Now, Mr Philby, what's this about a couple of my chaps not being able to go on the op?' he launched into the attack at once.

Philby was not in the least alarmed. 'Let's have a drink and make ourselves comfortable first,' he said, and signalled to one of the club's ancient frock-coated servants. 'Charles, a Scotch, a double, for me. And you?'

'The same,' Crooke muttered, 'with plenty of water.'

'I b-b-believe you know my father?' Philby said before Crooke could speak again.

'Yes, I met him briefly in the Middle East just before the war.'

'He is a queer old b-bird.'

Crooke did not reply, but Philby was right about the old man. St John Philby had gone native, in the late thirties. He had abandoned Christianity, become a Muslim, taken a Saudi slave girl as his second wife and acquired a 'bodyguard' of four huge mean-looking Abyssinian baboons.

'Funny,' Philby said, taking a deep sip of whiskey, 'although I-I've a fairly important job in the o-old firm, I couldn't g-get a security clearance for the old boy if I wanted to.'

'Why?'

'Because of the old chap's pro-fascist s-s-statements. In 1940 they p-put him inside for four months, you know. Eighteen B. Now I know my father is n-no Nazi. The authorities don't!'

Philby looked the typical product of a good public school and smart Oxbridge college, the kind the Secret Service always were eager to recruit. 'One of us,' Mallory would undoubtedly have said. Yet in spite of the man's obvious breeding and sincerity, there was that awful stammer. What did it indicate?

'Very interesting, Mr Philby. But what has all this got to do with my people and the operation?'

Philby was in no way offended by the sharpness of Crooke's words. 'It's basically the same with your chaps,' he said slowly. 'You can v-v-vouch for them. But the powers-that-be are not prepared to a-accept your word for it.'

'And who the devil are the powers-that-be?'

'*Me*,' Philby said calmly and signalled to the club servant to bring him another drink by holding up his matchbox horizontally. That obviously meant another double. Mr Philby was something of a toper, it seemed.

A stammerer who drank heavily. What nervousness did the two conceal? In spite of his almost permanent little smile, Crooke was beginning to distrust him. Charles left and Crooke went over to the attack again.

'Why?' he demanded, 'why don't you accept my word?'

'It's a very long and complicated story, Mr Crooke.'

'I'm ready to listen to a long and complicated story, Mr Philby.'

Philby nodded. He took another drink and, settling back more comfortably in the armchair, he began. 'Well, as you pr-probably know, Mr Churchill, for his own good reasons, doesn't want this country to bleed to death for the S-Soviet Union.'

'Quite rightly so,' Crooke said firmly.

'Of course,' Philby agreed. 'But our cousins across the sea, the Americans, don't quite g-go along with Mr Churchill. They maintain w-we must bleed for the g-good of our souls, democracy and W-Wall Street.'

Crooke noted the malicious smirk on Philby's face, as he said the last words, but he said nothing.

'Hence the op must remain secret from the A-Americans. They must believe that we are prepared to launch a Second Front this summer if the occasion arises.' He shrugged and finished his whisky. 'Your tame Yank can't go along. He ... might compromise the op.' 'And the German – Thaelmann?' Crooke asked, trying to keep his temper with this man who obviously knew nothing of the team spirit of the Destroyers in which nationality and political belief meant nothing.

Again Philby signalled for the servant. Another double. But there was no sign save a slight flushing of his cheeks that he was feeling his drinks.

'It's another l-long story, old chap, I'm afraid,' he continued when the servant had placed another drink in front of him. 'And I must remind you that this information m-must remain absolutely *entre nous*. Not even your chaps of th-the DNI must know.' He took a drink. 'Up to now I've been working for the SIS's I-Iberian section. But now that we've seen the boche off in Africa, I've been told by C ... *you know?*' He flashed an enquiring look at Crooke.

Crooke nodded. C was the head of the Secret Intelligence Service and the man who had sent them on their last mission. 'Well, C has in-informed me that I shall soon be working against the R-Russians.'

'*The Russians!*' Crooke blurted out in amazement, '*our allies!*' Philby smiled softly, obviously amused by the impact of his words.

'Erstwhile, old chap – erstwhile,' he said, his stutter suddenly gone. 'Who knows what may happen in another six months? They've had their victory at Stalingrad. They may well have another in the Caucasus. The Red hordes start their drive across Europe and the question arises, "where will they stop?" The Channel coast perhaps? You can see that we must exclude your communist too from the op. He could blow not just this op, but my whole new mission.'

Crooke forced himself to remain calm. 'My men wouldn't blow anything, as you call it, Mr Philby. I rely upon them utterly. You can too. Let me tell you a story. It won't be a long one.' Swiftly he sketched in the history of the Destroyers. How he had selected them from the jailbirds at Cairo's Military Prison, taken them 1,500 miles into the heart of the unexplored desert to prevent the Chief of Staff of the Egyptian Army from defecting to Rommel just before El Alamein. How, three months later, they had been parachuted into Nazi Germany to kill the Gestapo chief who had ordered the

33

slaughter of one hundred escaped POWs.

When he was finished, Philby nodded his head slowly. 'An impressive record, Mr Crooke, an impressive record, indeed.' Crooke pressed home his advantage. 'Don't you see,' he said, 'men like that can be relied upon in any situation regardless of their nationality or political belief! Every one of them is a loner. No family, no friends, always the threat of jail in the background if they slip up. In short, the only community to which they belong is the Destroyers. The Destroyers is their home, their family, their creed.'

Philby did not speak for a moment. Crooke stared at him anxiously, wondering if his pleas had done the trick. For the first time the slight look of cynicism in the Secret Serviceman's eyes had vanished. It was replaced by something which Crooke could only define as a look of understanding; as if Philby could well understand what he had meant by the Destroyers being loners, cut off from normal society by their records and their present employment. When Philby spoke again, his stutter had returned.

'All right, C-Crooke. They can go. But if you make a b-balls-up of this one, you're for the chop. Now then, let's get down to it.'

Over the next hour, Philby sketched in the background of the operation, interrupted every now and again by the creaking shoes of the elderly club servant bringing yet another double whisky. But in spite of his large consumption of alcohol, Philby did an excellent job of filling Crooke in on the Caucasian Fox. 'He was born in Konigsberg, East Prussia, 1902. He f-fought in the last German offensive in the west in-in 1918 and won the Kaiser's top decoration, the *P-Pour le Merite*. After the war he stayed on in the *R-Reichswehr,* in the Berlin 9th Infantry Regiment. Worked his way up the ladder till thirty-four when he spent four months in Dachau.'

'Why?'

'B-because he objected to the way the Nazis killed the former m-minister of war during the Roehm putsch. But he was too valuable apparently to be left in there. They h-hauled him out and as soon as Hitler started re-arming in '35, he s-started to shoot up the ladder. In Poland in '39 he commanded an i-infantry regiment. Six months later he was given a panzer division and was just beaten to the Channel Coast in the push across France by Rommel himself

35

with his S-Seventh Panzer. The rest you know. A very aggressive general, one of the best the Germans still have.'

From the person of the Caucasian Fox Philby took him to the site of their operation. 'The Caucasus lies between the Caspian and B-Black Seas,' he explained. 'It contains about nine million people divided into three republics, Georgian, Armenian and Azerbaydzhan. But they are republics in name only. The real power lies in Moscow's hands. Now, however, it's anybody's guess what's going on there. The Germans hold part of it, the Russians another, and in a sort of no-man's land in between the two armies, there are about fifty different linguistic groups trying to establish their own independence.'

'But how do we get in, if the terrain and conditions are as terrible as you portray them?'

'Good question. At first we thought the best way would be by air to Istanbul and then via the land route along the Turkish Black Sea coast. But that would take too much time and involve too many complications. Now we have decided on another route.' Crooke wondered who 'we' might be, but he did not interrupt. 'Instead of plane to Istanbul, you are now to fly as far as Malta and pick up a sub...'

'A sub?' Crooke echoed.

Philby grinned. 'I hope you don't suffer from c-claustrophobia?'

'I was just wondering how we would get through the Dardanelles. Surely the Turks will have slung nets across them as our people do at the approaches to Alex?'

Philby made a gesture of moving his forefinger across his thumb. 'Don't worry, we can oil the d-door of the Dardanelles. The Turks are friendly – at a price.' His grin vanished. 'The p-problem is to get out into the Black Sea. The Germans and the Russians are there in force – mostly subs and small fast boats – waiting for intruders to come out.' He shrugged and didn't finish the sentence.

'All right, so that's the risk we've got to take. What happens when we get through?'

'We've got to get you landed somewhere near the Caucasian Fox's HQ at Novorossiysk, where you'll be p-pleased to know we have a resistance g-group, who will help you if necessary.'

'Anti-German partisans?' Crooke queried.

Philby shook his head. 'No, anti-Russian,' he said carefully. Again he was pleased with the impact of his carefully sprung surprise on the one-eyed Army officer. 'You know, Crooke, we m-must be prepared.' He clicked his fingers at the ancient servant. 'Charles, the same again.'

When the drinks came, he raised his glass jovially to Crooke. 'Let's drink to the success of your op, Crooke – and to our noble R-Russian allies!' Then he giggled childishly. Crooke realised just how drunk Mr Harold Adrian Russell Philby was.

CHAPTER FOUR

Crooke walked, deep in thought, through the blackout down Gage Street towards the little flat that Mallory had organised for him in James Street. Since he had been working for the Directorate of Naval Intelligence these last twelve months, he had experienced a few eye-openers, but the SIS man's revelations had come as a real shock. For a long time he had been aware of the attempts of the nationalists within the Empire to pull the lion's tail, while the British were occupied fighting the Germans. But he had never realised just how seriously Mr Churchill took the danger presented by the Russians.

Far away to the south-east the sirens started to wail mournfully and the searchlights flicked on, poking their fingers into the darkness of the May night. But even the faint boom of the anti-aircraft guns and the pink stabs of flame on the horizon could not shake Crooke out of his reverie. A torch clicked on in a doorway.

'Hello, dearie,' a husky soft voice said,

'Fancy a bit tonight?'

An elderly whore stood there, the torch pressed against the base of her stomach, as she spread her legs and allowed the blue light to illuminate her ravaged face.

Crooke shook his head. It was a long time since he had had a woman, but since his wife had left him in Cairo in 1939 he had lost his confidence with the opposite sex.

'No,' he said slowly. 'No thanks!'

His words were drowned in a tremendous crash. The earth rocked and Crooke had a momentary glimpse of a large ball of blinding white light. Instinctively he ducked. The blast hit him in the face like a flabby warm fist and hurled him to the ground, an excruciating pain boring into his ears, his head ringing. When he struggled to his feet, the whore was gone, but her torch was still burning on the pavement. He picked it up and in a daze staggered down Royal Walk to the top of James Street. The street had been hit. Civilians were coming out of the wreckage, feeling their way with hesitant hands through the cloud of dust and acrid smoke. A group of dark shapes were bending over a figure lying on a heap of plaster rubble. Its breathing was harsh and laboured. The others seemed to be attempting to thrust a tube down its throat.

Suddenly an anti-aircraft gun fired from close by. The dark shapes jumped with shock. Momentarily a bright red flame illuminated the one holding the tube. Crooke caught a glimpse of the 'BELGIQUE' patch on the navy-blue uniform, and a pale face framed by bright red hair. It was the Wren who worked for Admiral Godfrey.

Up the street there came the roar of motors. An ambulance bell began to tinkle frantically. Crooke, wiping the thin trace of blood from his nose, staggered on. The Wren worked on, while someone in the darkness said over and over again. 'I told the old bugger he should have gone into the shelter. But he always knows better ... always knows better.'

Crooke turned into the house in which he had his flat on the fourth floor. He started to climb the stairs littered with plaster and broken glass. He paused on the landing of the second floor to catch his breath. The window had gone and he could pick out the momentary gun flashes, the ruddy glare of the flames and the uneasy searchlight waving its futility.

Wearily he plodded on. The third floor landing was heaped halfway up with debris, still smoking, the broken glass gleaming in the gun flashes which came through the holes in the ruined wall. With a grunt Crooke pushed away a fallen timber which barred his way. Suddenly he stopped and allowed the timber to fall back. A dark figure lay half-submerged in the debris. Crooke switched on the whore's torch. A girl came into view, her slim legs drawn up slightly beneath her black skirt, her white blouse setting off her trim figure. She lay in a gentle S, as if she were asleep, save for one thing – she had no head!

'This bloody futile war!' he cried out loud. 'Why?'

It was a question that would be echoed all over London that May night – all over the fighting world.

Suddenly he caught his breath. There was a soft tread above his head. It came from his own flat. He flicked off the torch, and very carefully began to make his way up the last flight, keeping to the edge of the steps where they didn't squeak. In the silences between the crashes of the anti-aircraft guns, he could hear the intruder quite distinctly now, as he moved back and forth.

'A burglar?' Crooke asked himself, as he clutched the torch like a truncheon. But what the devil did he expect to find in the flat, bare of everything save Crooke's spare uniform and a couple of cans of bully beef and biscuits? And what burglar would risk having his head blown off in a blitz to rob his pitiful little apartment? Instinctively Crooke knew that the intruder was no ordinary burglar.

At the door he paused. Then, drawing a long breath, he fitted his Yale key into the latch. Very carefully he turned it and opened the door. In the ruddy flickering light which came from the shattered window, Crooke saw a dark, khaki-clad figure crouched over the writing desk, a knife gleaming in his hand as he tried to force it.

The man was powerfully built. He could make out the muscled shoulders in the Ike jacket – and the high laced boots indicated that he had been trained as a paratrooper – an American paratrooper!

'What exactly are you up to?' he asked, flashing the blue light on the intruder.

The American turned.

Crooke caught a glimpse of a brutal animal face with eyebrows which grew almost together. Then the intruder's body flew through the air. Crooke was caught completely off his guard and together they tumbled to the littered floor.

Desperately Crooke squirmed to get from under the intruder's heavy bulk. He threshed his body from side to side while the other man bore down on him, knife upraised. With all his strength Crooke brought up his knee. It caught the American in the groin. He screamed and rolled back.

Crooke swung round and hit him hard with the side of his hand. He heard the nose-bone crack and his hand felt wet. Blood spurted from the American's broken nose.

'You bastard!' he said thickly.

As Crooke bent over, the American thrust out his forefinger. It struck through the black eye patch and penetrated deep into the empty socket. Crooke screamed with agony and fell back, clutching his face.

The American pressed home his advantage. As Crooke writhed on the floor, his hands clutched to his face, he rose and launched himself on the Destroyers, the knife gleaming in the ruddy light of the anti-aircraft guns.

Down on the ground, an unseeing Crooke lay completely defenceless. The paratrooper's jaw clenched as he prepared to deliver the death blow. But he was never to do so.

There was the vast hammer of sound as the bomb struck the house opposite. Great red-hot shards of razor-edged metal hissed through the air. The shrapnel caught the paratrooper in the small of the back. He screamed as it burned its way through the flesh. Fragments of bone and muscle slid down the opposite wall, splattering the shattered portrait of King George VI a gruesome red. Slowly the paratrooper's knees buckled below him. He sank to the floor – a hole as big as a fist in the small of his back. He was dead.

'A real old amateur job,' Stevens said scornfully, examining the broken window by the ruddy light of the fire burning in the opposite house, while Gippo ran his thin, brown fingers over the body of the dead American paratrooper. 'A blind man with two left hands could have got in this place, sir, without all that fuss and feathers. A bit o' sticky brown paper and bang. A nice clean noiseless hole. The stiff,' he indicated the dead man with a contemptuous nod, 'must have done it with his cap wrapped round his fist or something.'

'Thanks, Stevens,' Crooke said wearily, still sitting on the sagging bed and glad the two Destroyers had been able to get from their barracks so quickly when he telephoned. His empty eye socket still hurt like hell, but he forced himself to pursue the inquiry. 'Have you found anything, Gippo?'

Gippo held up a scrap of paper to the light from the outside. Far away to the west the first all-clear was beginning to echo mournfully; the German bombers in what the Londoners called the 'little blitz' were on their way back to the Fatherland. 'It says "Ger Embassy, Dub" – and what looks like a telephone number, sir.' He held up a ticket for Crooke on the bed to see. 'From Southern Ireland.'

'Anything else?' Crooke asked.

Obviously that was the way the American – if he was an American – had come in.

Gippo lowered his eyes and said 'No' softly.

'Come off it,' Stevens said aggressively. 'You bloody thieving nig-nog!'

He shook his head in mock disgust and said to Crooke, 'You just can't trust them, sir, you can't! Proper old tea leaves they are with their bloody black hands everywhere!' Crooke forced a smile at Stevens' outburst; he knew the two of them were as thick as – *thieves*. He completed the cliché to himself and laughed softly.

'What the devil are you talking about, Stevens?'

Stevens went over to Gippo and dug his hand in the other's hip pocket. It came out clutching a fat bundle of notes.

'Look at that, sir. Every one of them a pony.' He thrust the money under Crooke's nose in simulated anger. 'Blood money – to pay him for bumping you off, sir. And that wog wanted to keep it for himself. Can you beat it, sir!'

Crooke pushed the money away. 'Keep it and share it out among the lads. They deserve it.' He yawned suddenly. 'All right, I think you'd better get back to your barracks now. I'll see to him,' he indicated the body, 'in the morning.'

Gippo shuddered. 'You're not sleeping with the stiff one all night, sir?' he asked in alarm.

'Yes,' Crooke answered easily. 'Why not? He's dead.'

Gippo drew his long knife. 'No, sir, I'm not allowing it,' he said hotly in his fractured English. 'You cannot be trusting bodies.'

'He's right, sir,' Stevens said, 'even if he is only an ignorant wog. But it's not the stiff I'm worried about, it's them what's still alive. The blokes what put the finger on you.'

'You don't think it was just an ordinary burglary then?' Crooke asked.

'Gawd, no! You said yourself that you had nothing of any value here. Besides the yank there had all the dough he needed. Do you think he was after yer bully beef? No, sir, he was after you. That roll's blood money, as I said before.'

'But who "put the finger on me," as you put it?'

As the siren in Grosvenor Square took up the mournful dirge of the all-clear, Stevens said carefully, 'That's pretty obvious, sir, isn't it? The little foreign Wren from Naval Intelligence.'

CHAPTER FIVE

Philby, the MI6 man, led them through a maze of passages that the respectable façade of Number 21 Queen Anne's Gate concealed. The Destroyers and Mallory followed in silence, awed by the fact that they were in the heart of Britain's world-wide intelligence network, the HQ of MI6. They climbed up a short flight of steps, which brought them out on to the roof of the houses. Philby crossed a short iron bridge and led them into another maze, similar to the one they had just left. Finally he stopped in front of a door, blank of all signs, over which a green light was burning, obviously to indicate that whoever was in it was prepared to receive visitors.

Gently he tapped on the door. A faint voice said, 'Come.'

Philby poked his head around the door and said, 'They're h-here, C.'

Standing to one side, he allowed Mallory and the Destroyers to file by him and come to attention.

C, the head of MI6, took off his spectacles

and nodded to the Destroyers to stand at ease.

'Thank you, Philby,' he said, and nodded to Mallory. 'Commander, what about this business last night?'

Mallory, who did not particularly like C, made no attempt to hide the fact that DNI had been penetrated.

'Yes, you were right on the phone, C. The girl is a German agent. I checked her record. She came in in 1940 with the flood of refugees at the time of Dunkirk. She got a satisfactory and positive vetting by her own people in the Royal Victoria Patriotic. But of course at that time the country was swamped with refugees. Canaris obviously got some of his agents through then, sir.' Mallory believed that only God and the King should be addressed as 'sir,' but on this occasion he compromised. C was a very powerful figure with good connections at the Palace; it would be wise to keep him sweet.

'No doubt,' C said icily.

'For a year she worked with the Land Army and then in 1941 she volunteered for the Wrens – Signals. Good record there, according to my informant. That and her languages – Flemish, French, German and English – brought her to us in November last year.'

'And the American?'

'Deserter from an American airborne regiment stationed in Ulster. Went over the border last year just after they arrived in Europe. There he contacted the German Embassy in Dublin, perhaps through the IRA – they try to encourage Americans, especially Irish-Americans to desert. The ticket indicates he came across with a bunch of Irish labourers last month. Obviously he worked with the Belgian girl.'

C sniffed and raised his thin hand to pat the few wisps of grey hair that were left to him. 'Americans,' he said, 'funny lot. But I suppose they're better than no allies at all? So what's the drill now?'

Mallory looked at Philby.

'P-perhaps I can fill you in on that … sir?' he said. 'We m-must assume that the girl knows something of the Caucasian Fox op.'

'Must we, Philby?' C asked coldly. He flashed a look at Mallory. 'That doesn't say much for security in Naval Intelligence, does it, what?'

Mallory flushed. 'I'm afraid that's a question you must take up with Admiral Godfrey himself, sir,' he said, passing the buck neatly, but telling himself that one day he would hoist C with his own petard.

'Assuming that we're right about the girl kn-knowing,' Philby interrupted, using his stammer to advantage, 'then perhaps we can let BIA have a g-go at her, sir?'

C looked at the Destroyers as if he had noticed them for the very first time and explained. 'One of our sub-sections – the double-cross gang we call them among ourselves. They turn captured German agents and use them to feed fake information back to the twelveland.'

'But how exactly are you going to feed her false information without endangering us, sir?' Crooke asked.

'I think C-Commander Mallory and I could take care of that,' Philby answered for his chief. 'As I s-see it, you' – he indicated the Destroyers – 'will be dropped by parachute over the Baltic coast. There you will contact the Polish Underground – the Home Army – and they will conduct you over Poland into Russia, where you will execute your mission. That's the s-story we'll give the girl. Undoubtedly she h-has some form of c-contact with her masters in the *Abwehr*. P-perhaps through the Spanish Embassy or those double-dealing Swedes. At all events sh-she'll get it through to Canaris.'

For a moment C considered the suggestion. Then he nodded. 'All right, it sounds all right to me, Philby. But ensure that your security is watertight. As we have seen, Naval Intelligence is not too hot in that field. And while she's feeding Admiral Canaris with the false information, you intend to run these chaps' – he waves his hand at the Destroyers – 'in through the Black Sea, as we originally agreed?'

'Yes. The Admiralty has made the HMS *Dagger* available to us. It's in the Med already. The Admiralty signalled it this morning to sail for Malta to wait for our chaps,' Philby explained.

'I see,' C thought over his words for a moment. 'Well, Philby, it all seems to be in order. Have you any questions, Crooke?'

The leader of the Destroyers shook his head. 'No, sir. Mr Philby seems to have everything under control.'

C turned to Mallory. 'And you Commander?'

'No, everything is obviously in the capable hands of MI6. Nothing can go wrong, can it?'

C did not even notice Mallory's sarcasm. His sense of humour was obviously nil. 'Yes, Mallory, I think we've got the matter pretty well cut and dried,' he agreed.

'It's going to b-be an interesting e-exercise, sir,' Philby stuttered. 'The f-first time we've ever run anyone into Russia since the 1920s, if I am correct.'

'Yes, since the time of Dukes and Reilly,' C agreed. 'Now those were the days,' he added, his face warming a little as he thought of the time when the Secret Intelligence Service was obsessed with the 'red danger.'

'Yes, those w-were the days,' Philby echoed, a strange look in his soft eyes.

'Excuse me, sir.'

C looked at the Destroyers.

'Yes,' he said, as if he had suddenly remembered that they were still there. 'Yes?'

Stevens licked his lips a little uneasily. 'Well, sir, I've been thinking while you gentlemen have been talking that isn't all this business with the double-cross, or whatever you call it, not much use?'

'What *do* you mean?' C said disdainfully, turning his cold eyes on the red-faced cockney.

'Whatever we do, sir, regardless of the cover story you gentlemen dream up, one thing is for sure, sir,' Stevens persisted.

'And that is?'

'The Jerries'll be warned. Down in the Caucasus, they'll be waiting for us.'

CHAPTER SIX

The bearded skipper of HM Submarine *Dagger* shook Crooke awake. 'Zero four hundred,' he said heartily. 'If you want to have a dekko at the illuminations, you'd better rise and shine now.'

Crooke yawned and crawled out of the hammock crammed in above the youthful skipper's bunk. 'All right, thanks for waking me.'

'Don't mention it,' the skipper said cheerfully. He indicated the Destroyers sprawled in the gangway. 'If you want your tame thugs to have a look too, you'd better give them a shake.'

'Already awake,' Stevens said from the trembling metal deck. 'Couldn't kip in this bloody thing anyway – like a ruddy coffin.'

As the rest of the Destroyers started to wake up, Crooke followed the skipper to the periscope. Burton, who looked all of twenty, but who had served two years already in the Med and had a record of 50,000 tons of enemy vessels sunk behind him, adjusted the periscope and handed it over to Crooke. 'Over to port, Europe. On the other side, Asia,' he said.

Crooke took in the huge squat pile of St Sophia, the Suleiman mosque and the medieval wall which had failed to hold back the heathen hordes in the Middle Ages, then he handed the handles over to Stevens.

Stevens swung round the fabulous panorama at a shameless speed, then relinquished the periscope to Peters. 'First illuminations I've seen in four years, sir,' he said glumly. 'But not a bleeding houri in sight!'

Burton pushed his battered cap further to the back of his blond head. 'The usual drill would be to go through and into the Black Sea at night. That would give us plenty of cover. But there's a full moon and I have an inkling old Jerry, if he's waiting out there for folks like us, will be just about getting ready to take off for his home base and get out of Turkish territorial waters before the Turkish Navy starts getting too inquisitive.'

'I understand,' Crooke said. He liked the young officer. In spite of his extreme youth, he handled his forty-man picked crew and 200-foot-long boat, as if he had been doing it all his life. Mallory had really picked an expert this time. 'What exactly is the drill now?'

The skipper grinned. 'First thing is to dodge those bloody Turkish bumboats swanning around up there.' He referred to the many caiques which Crooke had spotted in the narrow channel between European and Asiatic Turkey. 'Once our Turkish friend has done his bit with the anti-sub nets, we'll swing north-east hugging the Turkish coast, but just outside territorial waters. The weather's favourable so we'll be able to cruise below the surface at about max speed – ten knots.'

'I see,' Crooke said and watched in amusement as Gippo suddenly let go of the periscope and staggered off to the latrine, his hand clutched to his mouth.

Behind him the Guardsman chuckled. 'It was those bumboats going up and down that did it.'

'Silly bugger,' Stevens said in disgust. 'Started to be as sick as a dog even before we got out of Valetta. Didn't even want to eat his bangers and mash last night.' He snorted and staggered after the half-breed. 'I'd better go and see what the stupid sod's up to, in case he flushes himself down the hole.'

It was a fine moonlit night. The Black Sea

had a heavy oily sheen. There was hardly any breeze and the Destroyers enjoyed the cool clean air after a whole day of being cooped up in the sub's stinking, hot interior.

Burton grinned at them. 'You can have a quick spit-and-draw if you like. But keep down under the cover of the conning tower. You'd be surprised how far even the light of a fag will carry at sea.'

Gratefully, Stevens pulled out a crumpled green packet of Woodbines and handed them round.

Crooke gazed at the dark line of the Turkish coast; beyond, somewhere in the gloom, was the Russian border.

'Penny for your thoughts,' Burton said.

'Not worth it. I wasn't even thinking. I was just enjoying the fresh air.'

'Fresh air! Can't compare with the smell of the old *Dagger*. After a while, you know, fresh air begins to stink.'

Crooke grinned. 'I'll take your word for it. But I think I'll stick to this stuff up here and leave you all you want of that stuff down there–'

Suddenly he stopped. From below there came a strange metallic pinging sound.

'What is that?' he began, but Burton did not give him time to finish.

'*Come on,*' he bawled, '*get below! all of you!*' He didn't wait for Crooke to move. He gave him a push towards the hatch.

Crooke staggered forward. Behind him a black shape appeared on the horizon, a white bone of foam in its teeth. A destroyer! The next few minutes flashed by in controlled chaos while the Destroyers crouched in the gangway trying to get out of the way of the sweating, hurrying sailors, taking the sub down in its frantic crash dive.

Then suddenly the frenzied action stopped. The ominous pings began to get louder. In the blue light the sailors' faces showed no emotion, but the sudden beads of sweat on their unshaven faces betrayed their inner tension.

The ping-ping rose in intensity. The sailors cramped in the narrow metal confines of the main compartment began to breathe with difficulty, as the carbon monoxide content in the air increased.

'Bloody hell,' Stevens said. 'What a sodding expensive coffin this is going to be!'

'Shut up!' Burton snapped with soft but firm authority. The skipper cocked his head to one side, as if he were listening. The whole sub was silent now. Every machine that made any kind of noise had been cut off. The planesmen and the helmsmen who controlled the electric motors had shifted to hand control. The sweat started to stream off their backs, staining their singlets black, as they fought to control the gigantic fins by the strength of their arms.

'Stand by for depth charge attack!' Burton roared suddenly at the top of his voice.

There was a click, followed by a gigantic clanging sound, as if the sub's hull had been struck by a massive sledgehammer. The whole sub rocked violently. A light bulb shattered over Thaelmann's head. He ducked instinctively. Cork, paint and tiny metal fragments flew through the air. A bald-headed petty officer with a boat tattooed on his naked chest grabbed the flood valve. If he opened it, compressed air would flood in and the sub would shoot to the surface.

'Destroyers at close quarters ... four different propellers turning,' the hydrophone operator called.

Crooke licked his lips and tried to drive out of his mind what would happen if one of the depth charges hit the sub. He looked round the faces of his men. They were unnaturally pale and tense; he knew they felt the same as he did.

But if Burton were scared, he did not show

60

his fear. As depth charge after depth charge exploded around the sub, sending it shuddering from side to side, he fought back with all the expertise he had gained from two years in the Med. While the crew fired waste oil, a collection of old clothes and a few odd fittings, already prepared for such an emergency, out of one of the torpedo tubes, he leaned over the hydrophone operator's shoulder trying to ascertain the position of the two destroyers somewhere above them. While he listened, he gave Crooke a running commentary over his shoulder. 'We could try to get a couple of miles away, surface and try to sit it out, but that's too dicey.' He stopped and listened intently for a moment. 'My idea is to try to bag one of the bastards.' He stopped again, the sweat pouring down his face. 'To do that, we've got to get up close enough … if we get him then we might be able to do a bunk in the confusion!'

He swung round to the petty officer with the bald head. 'Dan, take her up to twenty-five fathoms! We've got her!'

'Aye, aye, sir!' He released the valve.

As the sub shot upwards, the sweating sailor next to Crooke breathed a sigh of relief. Although he had only the vaguest idea of what was going on, Crooke felt he wasn't doomed to die at the bottom of the Black Sea after all.

Burton rapped out a series of orders. The Army men felt the boat shudder slightly as the outer doors of the torpedo tubes were opened.

'Stand by for final bearing,' Burton cried, hunched over the periscope. 'Mark bearing … set … fire one!'

The *Dagger* shuddered as the first torpedo left its metal nest.

'Fire two – and three!'

'Down periscope!' Burton yelled.

Suddenly everything was quiet again in the conning tower, but Crooke could see the men's lips moving noiselessly, as they counted the seconds of the torpedo run. Thirty seconds, sixty, seventy, eight-two, BOOM! They could hear the faint clanging sound of metal striking metal. It was followed by a series of small breaking noises, which Crooke knew would be magnified a thousandfold on the surface as the waters of the Black Sea started to pour in through the great jagged wound in the enemy's hull.

'Up periscope!' Burton cried, as the light of triumph flickered in the eyes of the waiting crew.

He peered into the glass. 'Spot on, lads!'

he yelled excitedly, without taking his eye away from the instrument, as if he could not see enough. 'Hit the bastard amidships! She's sinking fast. The other one is heading up to her. Bloody amateur to let himself be deflected like that. Should have continued the operation. If that skipper were in the Royal Navy, they'd court-martial him for dereliction of duty.'

'I hope the bloody German Navy gives him the Iron Cross – all three classes of it,' Steven said faintly and rubbed his hand across his drenched brow. 'Dereliction of duty, my arse!' Five minutes later they surfaced. Fortunately the moon had gone behind some sudden rain clouds. But the watchers on the bridge could just make out a dark lean shape cruising round in small circles about five hundred yards away. They didn't wait for an invitation to join in the rescue mission. The young skipper ordered the diesels started at once and rang down full speed. He ordered the generators to begin operating again to charge the batteries and the compressors which recharged the compressed air bottles. Down below the fans began driving fresh air through the boat.

Up on deck, Crooke watched as Burton took the submarine towards the rain squall on the horizon. Behind them came the angry squawk of a ship's siren, as the destroyer's captain realised that his prey had escaped him. But Burton took it calmly. In a matter of minutes they would be within the cover of the rain. 'Bye-bye, blackbird,' he said gaily, waving the end of his scruffy silk muffler at the faint outline of the destroyer. Crooke, watching him from the side of the conning tower, realised suddenly just how young Lieutenant J.W. Burton, RNVR was, but he had won his particular game of hide-and-seek. The prize for winning had been his life and those of the crew. But how long would he continue to win the game?

CHAPTER SEVEN

'Soviet Russia,' the Yank said maliciously, as he and Thaelmann sweated over the Cockle Mark II. 'The goddamn workers' paradise.' He spat contemptuously over the side of the stationary submarine.

Thaelmann looked up from the little canoe which the two of them were fitting out for their voyage to the shore some three miles away and said quietly, 'I'd be a little careful about what I said, if I were you, Yank.'

'Up yours!' the Yank replied roughly.

'Hey, you,' Peters butted in, pausing from his check of their personal weapons for a moment. 'Can't you knock it off? You'd think we were fighting each other and not the ruddy Jerries!'

Up above them on the conning tower, Crooke handed Burton his binoculars again. 'You think this is the place?'

Burton nodded confidently. 'Yes, it's the bearing the Admiralty signalled from London. Presumably they got it from your friend Mr Philby.'

In the white light of dawn there was little to be seen save a narrow strip of desolate coast with the Caucasian mountains beyond, their icy tips peeping through the top of the haze. To the left the narrow inlet lay, which could be the one that Philby had told them about in his briefing. But there was no sign of the welcoming committee the stuttering MI6 man had promised them would be there under its leader Loladze, chief of the anti-Russian Georgian partisan group.

Crooke hesitated. He had an uneasy feeling – that same uncanny emotion that had overcome him just before the abortive attack on Rommel's HQ in the desert. The inlet was a perfect place for an ambush. He bit his lip and wondered whether he should not wait a little, try to convince Burton to take the *Dagger* closer into the shore so that he could assess the situation a little more thoroughly. But then he dismissed the notion as quickly as it had come. He could not risk the *Dagger* and its crew. The Destroyers would have to take their chance as they always did. He bent over the edge of the conning tower. 'All right down there,' he ordered. 'Get your fingers out and let's get

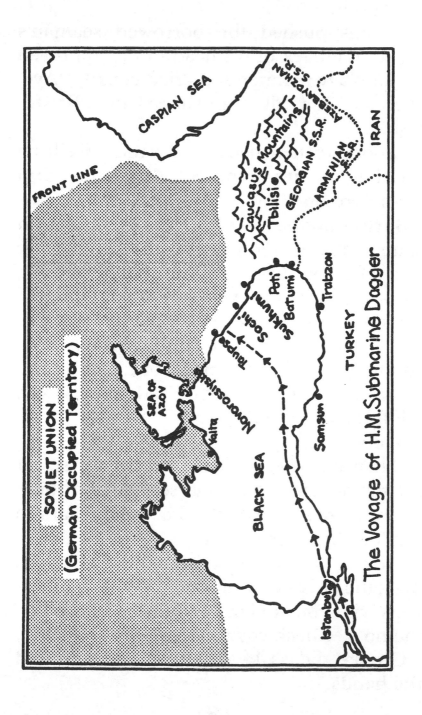

SOVIET UNION
(German Occupied Territory)

FRONT LINE

CASPIAN SEA

Caucasus Mountains

Tbilisi

GEORGIAN S.S.R.

ARMENIAN S.S.R.

AZERBAYDZHAN S.S.R.

IRAN

Poti

Batumi

Sukhumi

Sochi

Trabzon

Tuapse

Novorossisk

SEA OF AZOV

Yalta

Samsun

TURKEY

BLACK SEA

Istanbul

The Voyage of H.M.Submarine Dagger

on with it!'

Stevens pushed the borrowed seaman's cap to the back of his head in the approved Royal Navy manner and cried cockily, 'Aye, aye, sir. It's all ship-shape and Bristol fashion.'

Crooke turned back to Burton. 'We'll be off then in five minutes. What's the drill from here on?'

Burton nodded. Crooke could see that in spite of his proven bravery, the submariner was not too happy about being on the surface so long up where he was easy meat for any marauding German plane.

'As soon as you're under way, we'll submerge and wait at periscope depth until we get your signal that you've landed safely. We'll radio London then.'

'Good.'

'Then we'll head for the deeper water out there,' he indicated the sea behind him. 'Here we're sitting ducks. The water's far too shallow. Any German plane up top could see us.' He thrust out his wrist and looked at the big official-issue wristwatch. 'We'll rendezvous with you at eighteen hundred hours on the nose. Check your watch.'

Crooke did as he was told and adjusted the hands.

'If you've contacted your Russki friends by then, I'll signal their lordships and make my way back into Turkish coastal waters. We'll swan around there for a week.' He sniffed and tugged his beard. 'I don't think the Turks'll bother us much now that the wheels of progress have been greased. And we'll rendezvous again after dark on May 31st. Right? That is assuming you have completed your op successfully.'

'That sounds okay to me,' Crooke agreed.

Time was of the essence now. The sun was coming up over the snow-capped mountains. It hung on the horizon like a blood-red ball, a harbinger of the hot day to come. Already its first rays were beginning to burn away the mist over the land. Burton glanced anxiously to sea. As Crooke turned to clatter down the steel stairs to the deck, he said cheerfully, 'Don't worry, there's nothing out there. Beside, we're in Russian territorial waters.'

'Yes,' Burton said, 'but do the bloody Huns know that!'

Crooke began to rap out his orders to the Destroyers gathered around the Cockle Mark II, the official Royal Navy designation for the flimsy canoe which contained their gear. 'All right, lads, strip off. It's time to get mobile.'

The men needed no urging. They were only too glad to get away from the sub, in spite of the dangers that might lie ahead. None of them had proved particularly good sailors during the last few days, and the attack by the German destroyers had not improved their love of the sea. As Stevens had commented after they escaped from the Germans: 'They call the British a nation of sailors! Well, my mother must have done the dirty on the old man with a bloody Swiss!'

Swiftly they began to strip.

A great brawny-armed sailor, with blue and green tattoos covering his back, poised at the conning tower with brush in hand, painting in the *Dagger's* latest kill in the form of a destroyer, turned and cried in a fake falsetto: 'Oh look at them, nice soldier boys without their clothes on!' He pursed his unshaven lips and blew the Destroyers a kiss. 'I could really fall for that sweet little one in the middle.' The other sailors lounging on the deck joined in his hearty laughter.

Stevens clasped his hand to his hip and cried, 'Kiss me quick, me mother's drunk!'

The Yank, as surly and as aggressive as ever, glared at the big unshaven sailor with the dripping brush. 'Another crack like that, buddy,' he snarled, 'and you'll be a singing tenor in no seconds flat.' He touched the combat knife strapped to his hip to emphasise his words.

Swiftly they got out of their clothes and stowed them in the specially prepared waterproof rubber bags which they slung round their necks. The Guardsman and Gippo clambered awkwardly into the over-laden canoe. At the hoist, the bald-headed petty officer cried 'haul away,' and with a rattle of rusty chains the canoe was pulled into the air.

Crooke turned to Burton. 'Well, Skipper, thanks for the pleasure cruise – without the home comforts.'

'Nothing's too good for the boys in the Service,' Burton said casually. But the serious look in his eyes belied his easy flippancy. He grasped Crooke's hand and pressed it hard. 'All the best, Crooke.'

'Thanks. See you in seven days' time.'

Moments later the canoe had been deposited safely on the surface of the water and the other four Destroyers were slipping – one by one – into the sea after it.

As the canoe got underway, a slight swell blew up, throwing stinging salt spray into the Guardsman's face. Together with Gippo he began to strike out powerfully while the four Destroyers, hanging on to each side of the craft, helped the best they could with their legs. Behind them the sub crew prepared to dive. Suddenly there was a terrifying howl. Like a hawk pouncing on its prey from a great height, the dive bomber dropped out of the sky. The morning calm was ripped apart. The Destroyers stopped, hearts beating in alarm.

With a great roar the first dark blue plane came zooming in. When it seemed just about to crash headlong into the sub, the pilot, a dark blur against the gleam of the cockpit perspex, pulled out. Its radial motor screaming in protest, the plane roared upwards. Three little black eggs fell from its belly. They struck the sea a matter of yards from the *Dagger*. With a soft whoosh, three pillars of grey-green water flashed high into the air.

The Destroyers in the water ducked. A second later the wingman came roaring into the attack at 300 mph. Crooke caught a glimpse of the insignia on his wings. Two great red stars. The dive bombers were Russian! 'It's all right,' he shouted above the din and swallowed a mouthful of water.

'They're … Russian,' he spluttered. 'Mistaken identification!'

Burton had obviously spotted that they were Russian too. As the second load of bombs exploded about fifty yards away and the sub rocked wildly from side to side, he screamed something to the men on the swaying deck below. A barefoot rating pelted to the jackmast at the stern, obviously to hoist the white ensign. Burton himself grabbed his signal pistol. An instant later a series of white and green flares hissed into the sky and hung there motionlessly.

'It'll be all right,' Crooke gasped, searching the sky for the two dive bombers, which had zoomed high into the sun.

But it wasn't all right. Even before the flares had fallen to the sea, the two Stormovik dive-bombers roared in again.

Crooke shaded his eyes with his free hand, with the other hand hanging on to the canoe. The planes were black against the blood-red of the sun. 'Surely they can see the flag,' he yelled.

'Oh my Christ!' Stevens said softly.

A long sinister shape had detached itself from beneath the wing of the leading Stormovik. It hit the sea. For a moment a bone of foam rose from its nose, then it disappeared beneath the surface, a trail of bubbles tracing its path towards the stationary British sub.

On the conning tower Burton had seen it too. Frantically he rapped orders down the tube. They could see the young skipper's mouth move urgently but they couldn't hear the words against the roar of the two Russian planes.

Another torpedo slid into the water – and another. The Russians were directly above them now. They could see the red stars distinctly. Surely the pilots must see the white ensign! Suddenly, the sub erupted in a violent angry flame. Crooke caught a glimpse of Burton reeling back, his hand flashing to his face. Thick white smoke started to pour from the *Dagger's* stern. A great hiss like that of escaping steam burst out of its interior. Almost in the same instant the sub rolled over in the water like a giant metal whale turning on to its belly. A vicious ugly rent showed in its flesh. Water started to pour in. HMS *Dagger* began to sink.

Crooke pulled himself out of his horrified trance. '*Suction!*' he yelled above the roar of the sinking sub. '*Swim like hell!*'

The Guardsman and Gippo sprang to

their paddles. The men in the water kicked out their feet aggressively. The little canoe rushed forward. As he gasped for breath, Crooke glanced behind him at the sinking submarine. A few black heads were now bobbing up on the surface. Pathetic little bits and pieces of gear started to emerge. A thick explosion came from within the dying ship. Great bubbles of air gouted up, mixed with the cries of the panic-stricken survivors. Tank after tank exploded below the surface. The *Dagger* jerked uncertainly as she fought against gravity, belching bubbles all the while. To no avail. Her sharp bow pointed straight into the sky. Almost gracefully she accepted her fate and slid to the bottom of the Black Sea.

But their ordeal was not yet over. The two Stormovik divebombers came in line abreast for a third time. Their bombs and torpedoes were gone now. But they still had their machine-guns. They came in slowly, taking their time, waggling their wings like birds in spring, enjoying their power and their invulnerability. Almost casually the machine guns in their wings began to crackle. Tracer zipped over the surface of the water.

'Oh, my God,' the Guardsman cried, his paddle poised in his hand almost stupidly, 'they're machine-gunning the poor bastards!'

The Yank reacted first. He leaped out of the water and grabbed the Guardsman. Together they crashed back into the sea. The little canoe rocked violently. As Gippo fell over the side, it overturned completely and spilled most of its contents into the water.

The American had acted just in time. One of the dive bombers broke away in a lazy curve and bullets began to wing their way too. They ducked hastily, swallowing water in their panic. Time and again, the two Russians swept over their heads spraying the survivors with bullets. A body bumped into Crooke as the debris floated into them. It was that of the bald-headed petty officer, his face black with oil, a neat red hole drilled in the centre of his forehead like an extra mouth. He moved aside and let it bob on. Then at last the cold-blooded murder of the survivors was over, and the roar of the planes died away.

Crooke stuck his head above the surface of the water. Already they were two black dots in the distance, winging back to their home base. A moment later and they were gone.

Shocked into silence, the Destroyers trod water and stared about them as the flotsam bumped back and forth – airtight tins of duty-free cigarettes, ratings' caps, a half-empty bottle, a couple of carlin floats, life jackets – and bodies. Many bodies! Sadly they righted the canoe and saved what they could while the others helped the Guardsman and Gippo to clamber back in again.

'Why?' Stevens asked, posing that old old question about the gratuitous brutality and futility of war that men have always asked at such moments.

No one could give him an answer. Sapped of emotion and with no heart for their task, they began to paddle towards the shore.

'But surely Mr Philby would have warned them we was coming sir!' Stevens persisted.

'Mr Philby?' Crooke said hollowly, 'I can't answer that one for you, Stevens, I'm afraid.'

They paddled on. The shore of the Soviet Republic of Georgia grew closer and closer, but Crooke had no eyes for it. His mind was too occupied with Stevens' question; that tremendous overwhelming 'why.' But as the little Cockle Mark II started to approach the tidal race, he had to drop it from his mind and concentrate on the task at hand.

Twenty years would pass before Stevens' question would be answered and by then

Crooke's body had long since rotted away at the bottom of the Suez Canal, trapped in the shroudlines of his own parachute.

SECTION TWO:
THE CAUCASIAN FOX

'So that's your Caucasian Fox... If all Germans were like that they would have won the war in Russia in 1942.'

The Circassian Banu to Lt. Crooke

CHAPTER ONE

The heat waves rippled on the naked plain. The dust lay inches deep. Every time they put a foot down, a little cloud rose to obscure their legs. The sweat streaming down their faces in the white glare of the sun, their thin civilian shirts soaked black, they plodded on.

'I must have a sodding ton of that bloody dust in my guts,' Stevens cursed and shifted the bag containing the plastic explosive to his other shoulder.

The Yank at his side, carrying their only sten, which he had rescued the day before from the sea, licked his grey mouth. Abruptly his lips gleamed a bright red against the dust. 'When I was a young 'un on the ranch,' he grunted, 'my daddy used to say that a steer needed a couple of pounds of dirt in its guts to be able to crap all right.'

'Well, I'm no f-ing cow,' Stevens commented drily.

At their head Crooke, sucking a pebble, the old desert remedy against thirst, spat it out and called: 'All right, lads, let's take five.'

They needed no urging. They flopped down where they were, not even bothering to take the waterproof bags, which contained all they had managed to salvage, from their shoulders. Momentarily a thick cloud of dust rose and obscured their view. As Crooke wiped his forehead with the back of his arm, the dust cloud slowly began to settle again. He narrowed his eye against the glare. The horizon, framed by the snowy peaks of the mountains, was empty. It was like some moon landscape, devoid of any life save for the lizards which scuttled through the parched shrubs.

It had been the same the day before when they finally forced the canoe through the tidal race into the inlet. There had been no welcoming committee to receive them as Philby had promised. Perhaps the intelligence man had slipped up; perhaps the partisans had been captured. But no one had shown up all that day while they waited anxiously in the burning sand dunes. In the end when dusk had fallen on them, Crooke decided they could wait no longer. Ordering the Destroyers to collect the bits and pieces of operational gear which they had managed to salvage from the water, he had moved out.

All night they had marched north, sticking as close as they could to the coast, plodding on hour after hour, moving through the Georgian wasteland, empty of all life. It had been the same after the sun had risen with dramatic bloodred suddenness of the Orient. There had been no sign of Philby's promised pro-British partisans – or of anyone else.

Once they had dropped to the ground as a cloud of dust rose on the horizon but their alarm had been unnecessary. The cause had not been man, but a group of wild animals. Now they had been marching doggedly northwards for over fourteen hours without seeing a human being or any indication that human beings had ever inhabited the Soviet Republic of Georgia.

'Listen,' Crooke said thickly, staring round at them as they lay in a semi-circle in the dust, 'I imagine you have all realised by now that we're in a pretty sticky situation.'

'Right up the creek – without a paddle,' Stevens agreed. 'The Jerries know we're coming and that Mr Philby has dropped a real old goolie. Him and his sodding resistance group!'

Thaelmann sighed. 'Didn't I say that it

was all bourgeois wishful-thinking. A survival of the past. Whatever their races, the people of Soviet Russia have accepted Mr Stalin.' He said the words heavily, as if they bored him.

'Makes no goddamn difference,' the Yank cut in irritably and spat expertly at a lizard which had poked its head out of the dust and begun to stare at the intruders. It fled hurriedly. 'We've been spat on from a great height. The question now is what we're gonna do?'

'We've got two possibilities open to us. We're probably about two hundred miles from the Turkish border. We could try to make it back there.'

'And have them stupid sods in Intelligence with all their mumbo-jumbo giving us a hard time,' Stevens objected. 'Not on your nelly!'

Crooke nodded in approval. Stevens was right. He had always thought that there was something childish about officers connected with Intelligence. The 'keyhole complex' he called it to himself: their infantile desire to know what was going on the other side of the door.

'What's the alternative, sir?' Peters asked.

'To go on with our mission.'

'We haven't much to go on with,' Peters said. 'The clothes we stand up in, the Yank's sten, Gippo's carving knife and two revolvers – plus the plastic explosive.' He glanced at the naked burning plain with its patches of withered scrub, bent by the prevailing wind. 'Not much to go on with.'

Crooke took his eye away from the tortured landscape. 'You're right, Peters. It doesn't look as if anyone has lived here since Noah landed with his ark over there.' He pointed in the general direction of Mount Ararat. 'However, Mr Philby said there are people here somewhere. Naturally a lot fled when the Germans came. The menfolk went up into the mountains where they were safe and could keep their herds from the soldiery of both sides. But the women stayed behind. According to Mr Philby again, they go underground for most of the winter, burrowing into the slopes of the foothills facing the sea. The temperature falls to forty degrees in the winter – *minus.*'

'So we hope to find one of their villages, sir?'

'Yes, that's the general idea. That's why I don't want to get too far from the coast. But,' he hesitated and looked around at their dust-caked faces, 'it's up to you what we do.' Stevens rose wearily to his feet and slung his bag once more.

'Bints and grub – that's as good a reason as any, sir,' he said with renewed confidence. 'I'm with you, sir.'

Crooke looked at the others. They were not going to let him down.

It was furnace hot. The glare sliced at their eyes like a sharp blade. The white light striking the stone-littered surface of the plain quivered tremulously. Above them the heavy motionless sky was the colour of wood smoke. Through it the sun appeared like a copper penny seen at the bottom of a dirty pond. But the Destroyers noticed neither the heat nor the glare. They were concerned solely with the holes dug in the hillside ahead of them from which little puffs of smoke emerged as if it were a volcano preparing to explode.

Crooke broke their concentration. 'It looks pretty easy,' he said at length. 'A couple of us at the base of the hillside in case they try to run down it, the rest of us coming in from both sides.'

'What about the top of the hill, sir?' Peters queried.

'No deal,' the Yank answered for Crooke.

'They won't be able to get up there quick enough. If they try to make a run for it, they'll head downwards.'

Crooke agreed. 'You're right. But let's give them another thirty minutes or so. My guess is they'll start cooking their evening meal soon, before the sun goes down. Let's try to catch them while they're busy with the food.'

While the burned brass of the sun moved steadily westwards towards the sea behind the next range of parched hills, the Destroyers watched the lazy movements of the villagers. Once an old man dragged together a great bunch of the dry shrub, using a wooden rake – presumably to be used for the cooking fires. A little later a pot-bellied, barefoot boy waddled out and grabbed one of the skinny chickens which ran around outside by the scruff of the neck and carried it squawking back into the caves. Then the little plateau at the base of the primitive village was empty, given over to the chickens and a sleeping dog. Ten minutes later they moved in. Everything went according to plan. They surprised the villagers over their cooking pots, as Crooke had hoped they would do. Coughing in the thick wood smoke which filled the caves, they forced the terrified villagers outside.

Apart from two ancient men whose faces were gnarled like dark walnuts, the little community consisted of a dozen or so women, their figures ruined by too much child-bearing to which the score of dark-eyed, pot-bellied children clinging to their long skirts testified. By dint of much arm-waving and a few prods with their sticks, they herded the women together into the centre of the little plateau.

'What now?' Stevens asked, grabbing a half-cooked leg of chicken from one of the pots as he passed it.

'Put that back,' Crooke commanded.

While a sullen Stevens dropped the chicken leg back into the pot, Crooke pointed to the woman immediately in front of him, her pendulous breasts hanging loose beneath a tight flowered jacket, with a pair of baggy pants tied at the ankles, peering out from under her dirty apron. 'Come here,' he ordered, waving his hand at her.

The old woman showed a mouthful of rotten yellow teeth and shrugged in incomprehension, but her original look of abject fear had vanished for some reason.

The Yank shoved her forward brutally. 'Haul ass, you old cow!' he snarled.

'Leave her alone,' a cold voice said in good English, 'and please put up your hands!'

The Destroyers swung round. Then, one after another, they began to raise their hands as ordered.

A woman of about thirty was standing behind them, a Russian machine gun under her arm. With an abrupt movement of her head she threw her long gleaming black hair back and said, 'You – with the gun.' She indicated Thaelmann, who had the team's sten, 'Drop it!'

He did as he was told.

For a moment no one spoke. Crooke studied the woman. She was too generously built for English tastes, but there was no denying the animal provocativeness expressed by her every movement, as she came closer.

Calmly, as if she met strange Englishmen in the middle of the Georgian wilderness every day, she said. 'My name is Banu – that means Lady in English. I'm Circassian. We are all Circassian here.'

Crooke felt a sensation of relief. They hadn't walked into a German trap after all. 'Then you are Russian?' he said. She shrugged in the Oriental manner, her large breasts moving easily under the thin flowered material of her blouse. 'In name... But no more.' She shifted the position of the machine gun. 'But who are you?'

'We're British soldiers,' Crooke said, explaining their civilian clothes by touching the two plastic identity discs around his neck.

'You have come to rescue us?' she said.

'From whom?'

She nodded at the tattered poster stuck to the rock. 'From him.'

In the fading light, Crooke could make out the face he had seen a thousand times or more in the newsreels in these last few years. It was that of the broad-faced, moustached, cunning-eyed Marshal who had been Britain's ally for the past eighteen months, the man everyone was now calling 'Uncle Joe' – Josef Stalin. As Crooke stared at the poster, Gippo dropped on the woman from the ledge, still clutching a looted piece of bread in his hand.

It was not easy to calm her. But Peters' obvious sincerity and the way he came between the Circassian woman and the Yank's brutality seemed to convince her that the Destroyers meant no harm to her and her people; for she was undoubtedly the spokesman of the illiterate hillside villagers. Gradually her defiance died away and as the Destroyers ate the strange sweet-sour chicken dish the frightened peasants set before them, she told them her story. 'Until last year I was an assistant in the English Seminar of the Karl Marx University at Tiflis, the capital of Georgia. I was going to be a professor. Then the Germans attacked on the Terek and we all fled. I came back to my people. Here I knew I was safe.'

'Safe from the Germans?'

'The Germans, the Russians, the Georgians, the Armenians–' she pouted contemptuously, and swept her hand round the circle of villagers staring at them in the flickering yellow light of the tallow candle. 'Once they were the aristocrats of the Caucasian region. Every seventh man noble-born. When the Communists came in 1920, we fought and then fled into Turkey. But the Turks did not want us, for we were Christian. They forced us back over the border. Now with the central control from Moscow gone, every man's hand is against us. All of them want to – how do you say in English? – pay back an old–' she fumbled for the correct word.

'An old score,' Crooke prompted.

91

'Thank you. Yes. So now all the other nationalities are against us. In the Caucasus in 1943, it is the time of the long knife.' She made an energetic gesture, as if she were thrusting a dagger in someone's back. 'We Circassians have only ourselves to depend on.'

'But where are your menfolk?' Peters asked, picking up the bowl of thick dirty-white yoghurt which the old crone with the baggy pants had given him.

'They are up in the mountains with the herds. They will stay up there till winter – until it is safe to come down again. All we have is the two old ones.' She pointed to the two ancient men at the back of the semi-circle of gawping faces, staring at their sudden visitors in blank incomprehension.

Stevens nudged Gippo. 'I wouldn't mind keeping her back warm for her all winter–' His words ended in a gulp as he swallowed the first spoonful of the thick yoghurt. 'What the hell is this?' he said.

'It will make you strong and virile,' Gippo answered swallowing his greedily. 'You will live to be a hundred, if you eat it regularly.'

'Not on your nelly,' Stevens snorted in disgust. 'Not if I have to eat this pap!'

The woman laughed at his disdainful

expression, as he put down the earthenware bowl and turned to Crooke once more. 'But I have talked enough. Tell me about yourselves. Why are you here?'

Crooke knew he could trust her. Besides, he knew he needed her help, if he were going to carry out the mission successfully. 'We must get to Novorossiysk,' he said, 'and soon.'

'Why?'

'To kill someone.'

'A German or a Russian?'

'A German.'

Banu's face fell.

'And Russians too – or anyone else who tries to get in our way.' Crooke added hurriedly.

Like all Orientals her emotions were direct and unconcealed. Her face brightened at once. '*Then*, I'll help you.' Hurriedly she got to her feet. 'Let me get the map.'

CHAPTER TWO

'It's the only map I have,' she said, apologetically, as she spread the tattered piece of paper on the dusty floor and the Destroyers squatted around her in the light of the candle. Outside it was completely dark now. From far away a wild dog was howling at the night. 'We are here,' she stabbed her finger at a point on the coast of the Black Sea. 'You want to get there.'

'Proper old school teacher, isn't she?' Stevens whispered to Gippo.

'Me she could teach things – without doubt,' he answered and made a crude gesture with the forefinger of his right hand and the clasped thumb and forefinger of the other.

'Between the two places there is perhaps three hundred kilometres,' she continued, 'or maybe a little less to the German first defensive line – what they call the "blue line".' She indicated the area on the map.

'So the rest is in Russian hands?' Crooke asked.

She shook her head. 'Not really. We are between two fronts in an area inhabited by fifty or sixty different nationalities, speaking languages as different as Arabic is from English. Each race tries to look after itself the best it can, but on the coast it is the partisans who are in charge.'

Crooke pricked up his ears. Were these men the ones Philby had talked about so confidently in Queen Anne's Gate? 'Partisans?' he asked.

'Partisans – they call themselves, the patriots! *We call them bandits!* They have guns and money from Moscow for doing little except attacking our villages, forcing our men to join them in the woods – and taking our women, when there is no man to stop them. But one day we shall have our revenge on Loladze and his bunch of bandits.'

'How do you suggest we try to reach Novorossiysk?' Crooke asked, trying to keep her to the task at hand. 'The coast?'

'Yes,' and with her finger she traced a line along the winding Black Sea coast. 'We follow the coast, staying in my people's villages. Then–'

'*We?*' Stevens interrupted, as usual quicker off the mark than the rest of the Destroyers.

'Yes,' she answered, 'you and I.'

'But you're a woman,' Crooke protested. 'Besides, you'd be risking your life if the Germans catch us.' He indicated his rough civilian clothes. 'They could shoot us – as spies.'

Her face did not change. 'I have a reason too for going to Novorossiysk,' she replied. 'When you have dealt with your German,' she added, as if it were the most reasonable thing in the world, 'You will help my people to get rid of the Russian bandits, no?'

They set off at dawn the next morning. The whole village insisted on embracing them and handing them packages of cold chicken, flat unleavened bread and the ubiquitous yoghurt. Crooke offered the old woman with the yellow teeth, who appeared to be in charge of the little community, two of the gold sovereigns which they had brought with them on Philby's advice. But she refused them indignantly and then insisted on embracing him once more.

The next five days were spent in hard marching during the daylight and equally hard celebrating after nightfall at one of the Circassian villages which dotted their route. Replete with *schihirtma,* a kind of sweet-sour chicken, or something that looked like a bowl of porridge covered with a red sauce and turned out to be deboned chicken, beaten to a pulp and prepared with walnut oil, they set off each dawn, their heads still heavy from the *raki* of the night before.

They followed the old Anglo-Indian cable line which ran from Calcutta via the Caucasus to Britain. Once it had been a symbol of British power, reporting everything of importance from Delhi to London, from the death of Edward the Seventh to the outbreak of the Second World War.

Occasionally they would spot groups of men on the horizon, but whether they were German or Russian they had no time to find out. Banu would order them to flee into the nearest patch of six-foot high sunflowers, now growing wild since the local farmers had fled; and there they would wait until she felt the danger was over. There was no denying the woman's toughness and ability. She insisted on keeping up the same pace as the Destroyers, and when the Guardsman offered to carry her bundle, she refused scornfully, saying, 'In the old days, we Circassians were Cossacks and more often than not the women rode to war with their men.'

As Stevens commented softly and in admiration to Crooke: 'I think we'd better make her an honorary member of the Destroyers, sir. She'd be an improvement on that dirty nignog at least.'

On the sixth day it was obvious they were coming closer to the real front. The barren fields on both sides of the track were littered with the rusting debris of the previous year's battles: burned-out tanks and trucks, shattered guns, abandoned furry-backed German packs and here and there the gleaming white skeletons of horses from which heavy-bellied crows rose slowly as they approached.

That afternoon they were resting in the shade of a sunflower field when Gippo and Stevens, who as usual had been out scrounging among abandoned German equipment, came running, crying, 'Jerries coming, sir! *Scarper!*'

Urgently they backed into the tall dry stalks, closing them individually as they penetrated deeper into the field, so that a casual observer would not be able to spot their tracks. They flopped to the ground, hearts beating frantically, and peered along the ground at the long earth-brown worm of men slowly winding their way up the track towards them, a soft hum preceding it.

'They're Russians, sir,' the Guardsman whispered to Crooke.

'Yes, POWs, look there – that half-track! That's German all right.'

The prisoners came closer. Six abreast, they staggered and stumbled over the littered track in the burning heat, misery in their dark eyes, the sweat pouring down their shaven skulls and on to their emaciated faces. In the half-tracks, the Germans, bare-headed and very much at their ease, urged them on with hoarse shouts and the occasional cuff about the head when one of them seemed about to stagger out of line. The prisoners came parallel with the hiding Destroyers.

'Goddam!' the Yank gasped. 'What a helluva stink!' He closed his mouth swiftly.

The stench came from the wretched POWs and reminded Crooke of the zoos of his youth: a combination of the filthy odour of the monkey house and the biting urine stink of the mangy captive lions. But these were not animals but men, kept upright and moving by some last flicker of will.

Finally they passed. Stevens breathed a sigh of relief. 'Bloody hell, am I glad those buggers have gone. Smelled like the inside of a gorilla's armpit they did!' Stiffly he started to get to his feet. Banu grabbed him hastily. 'Keep down,' she said urgently.

Then Stevens heard the faint noise of the tank motor as well and dropped to the ground again. Five minutes later the great camouflaged Ferdinand self-propelled gun came level with them, driven in low gear. On both sides tense *panzer grenadiers,* machine pistols over their arms as if they were hunting, stalked on foot while on the burning metal deck of the vehicle a sharp-eyed corporal crouched over twin Spandaus ready to go into action at once. This was the German rearguard.

Banu crawled closer to Crooke. 'Look,' she whispered, as the Ferdinand rattled by. 'Over there.' On the hill in the far distance a low cloud had made a sudden appearance. 'Partisans,' Banu said.

'Cavalry!' Stevens gasped, as they grew nearer. 'Christ, this is like Tom Mix!'

The German *panzer grenadiers* spotted the partisans at the same moment. On the deck of the Ferdinand the twin Spandaus sprang into action. Their high-pitched burr broke the afternoon's heavy silence. Gleaming brass cartridges tumbled noisily to the metal deck. The Ferdinand stopped with a sudden lurch. Hastily the *panzer grenadiers* clambered aboard.

Banu nudged Crooke. 'Look over there.'

He followed the direction of her gaze. Across the track dark figures were moving through the sunflowers. Bending down then darting forward a few feet, they advanced on the unsuspecting Germans like a pack of brown wolves. There was something uncanny about the approach of this new enemy.

'Now watch,' the Circassian woman said, as if she had seen this all before and was presenting it for their entertainment. The partisan cavalry broke into two groups, spreading out in two horns on both sides of the self-propelled gun. The corporal saw at once that the enemy was trying to cut him off. The time had come to move. And quickly. While his men fired frantically at the cavalry, he bellowed an order to the unseen driver.

The SP lurched forward towards the other field of sunflowers. Already, Crooke could guess, the radio operator was tapping out a frantic code message for assistance to the column ahead of them. It came to a sudden halt with the apparent protection of the high sunflowers behind it. The *panzer grenadiers* dropped over the sides and took up their defensive positions as the cavalry on their shaggy, ragged-maned brown horses came closer. Their fire discipline was excellent now that they had overcome the first shock of the surprise attack. They let the partisans come closer and closer. Obviously the corporal was saving his ammunition.

Suddenly the Russians in the sunflower field burst out of their hiding places. The corporal swung his twin Spandaus round and fired. A row of brown figures fell to the ground, bowled over as if by some gigantic invisible hand. The rest came on. The field teemed with the partisans. Frantically the handful of Germans tried to stop them. They fired wildly into the advancing mass. The great gun itself shivered and an 88mm shell went roaring over the attackers' heads. Everything was chaos, the air full of the screams of wounded and dying and the crackle of small arms fire. And then the Russians swamped the *panzer grenadiers*. A few last shots, a final scream of agonized pain and it was all over. From both flanks now the cavalry came charging in, the riders screaming with triumph at their victory, galloping heedlessly over their own dead and dying, the blades of their sabres gleaming in the sunlight. Seconds later the Ferdinand disappeared from sight in the excited mass of partisans.

'Wow,' the Yank breathed, 'now what da ya say to that?'

'They are Russians,' Thaelmann said proudly. 'They know how to fight.'

'They sure do that!' the Yank agreed with unusual enthusiasm.

'And they are bandits too,' Banu said bitterly.

'What do you mean by that?' the Guardsman said. 'They're our Allies, miss.'

'Just you wait and see,' she replied.

'Banu is right,' Crooke said cautiously. 'Just let's see what happens before we reveal ourselves. After that business with the dive bombers, I think we'd better recce the situation a bit. We don't know who this bunch are, after all.'

Banu nodded cynically. 'You will soon find out, believe you me.'

Hidden in the sunflowers, the Destroyers could see the German prisoner trembling all over. When the partisans pulled him to his feet, his legs would not support him and two bearded Russians had to hold him under the armpits.

The big leader in the black leather jacket rose from the fire and stepped forward. Now that he and his men had celebrated their victory, he was ready to interrogate the sole survivor at his leisure. Obviously the dead German corporal had not been able to contact the rest of the column so the Russians had time.

He said something to the German.

Dumbly the latter shook his head.

Very calmly the partisan leader pulled a long knife from the top of his riding boot. Slowly he brought it level with the German's eyes. He jerked his head back, but still he did not answer the partisan's question. The black-jacketed leader nodded calmly to the two bearded men. Each freed a hand and grabbed the *grenadier's* hair. The partisan thrust out his hand and seized the German's left ear. A scream which did not seem to originate from a human being tore through the still evening air.

'Oh my bloody Christ,' Stevens moaned, 'he's cut off the poor bugger's lug!'

'They want information,' Thaelmann said thickly. 'This is not kid-glove war–'

His words were cut short by another agonised scream – and another. Banu covered her ears with her hands and closed her eyes tightly. Crooke caught a glimpse of Gippo, his knuckles pressed between his teeth, the sweat pouring down his dark forehead.

The screams of ágony seemed to go on forever as the black-coated leader systematically tortured the young German prisoner. Then finally they gave way to sobs, a few last whimpers and silence, as the German slumped to the ground, released from the terrible pain by death itself.

An hour later the partisans left after stripping the Ferdinand of what they could take with them and fussing over the dead bodies of the *panzer grenadiers* for reasons known only to themselves. The leader clambered on to his pony and gave the signal to move out. As he did so, the Destroyers caught a glimpse of the weapon slung over his back.

'Hey, get a load of that,' the Yank cried. 'That's one of your limey sten guns. Now where in hell's name did he get that?'

But no one could or would answer his question. Their attention was riveted on the partisans disappearing the way they had come like some strange Hunnish horde of ancient times.

When they had finally disappeared into the night and the beat of their ponies' hooves could no longer be heard, Banu broke the silence. 'That was Loladze,' she said, 'the partisan leader and the man who murdered my father.'

CHAPTER THREE

'Jesus, just look at the poor bugger,' Stevens breathed. 'Both his ears are gone!'

'What's that in his mouth?' Thaelmann asked in awe.

'Cover him up,' Crooke snarled. The man's bloodstained fly told him all he needed to know.

None of the other Destroyers seemed able to move; they stood rooted there staring down in fascinated horror at the mutilated soldier. So Crooke himself seized an abandoned German cape and flung it over the dead man.

Slowly like automatons they approached the dead *panzer grenadiers* who lay where they had been killed, their faces already a waxy white against the mottled green of their camouflaged jackets.

'Poor bastards look like the bloody wax-works at Madame Tussauds,' Stevens said.

The Destroyers stared down at the dead Germans. One was squatted near the earthen bank, his ruined machine pistol still clasped in hands which were already rigid. Another lay on his back, while a third crouched in the ditch, the blood black and hard on the side of his face.

'Don't move!' Crooke broke into their reverie. 'Everybody stop where he is.'

The urgency of his order made them freeze. They stood as stiff and tense as the dead grenadiers all round them.

'All right,' Crooke continued, 'watch your step. They've mined the bodies! Look over there!' Cautiously he picked up a stick and poked the nearest body. In the fading light of the camp fire they could see the little round personnel mine hidden beneath it.

'Pretty damn neat – pretty damn neat,' the Yank commented bitterly.

'Yes, I've seen it before in the desert,' Peters said. 'The Eyeties did it to our dead in '40. When the Sappers tried to lift the bodies, they got one of those things in their face.'

Crooke nodded. 'It's an old trick and not a very pleasant one. So be careful the lot of you. All right, Gippo and Stevens, you two check that SP out – and you, Gippo, keep your fingers off the bodies. They won't stay long otherwise, you understand?'

'Yessir, Captain, I understand,' Gippo

answered as he and Stevens made their way cautiously to the SP.

A few minutes later Stevens had managed to get inside the Ferdinand safely. Cautiously he pressed the starter while the others held their breath in case it was booby-trapped too. But it wasn't. A moment later the SP's two great 530hp twin Mayback engines thundered into noisy life. On the turret, Gippo raised his thumb in triumph and flashed a grin at them. 'Come on,' he yelled above the roar, 'we're going!'

The Destroyers needed no urging.

'Now ya cooking with gas,' the Yank yelled joyfully. 'I'm sick of hoofing it.'

Minutes later they were aboard and rumbling through the darkness towards Novorossiysk.

Five hours later, with Banu's help, they passed through the German Blue Line. It turned out not to be a continuous front but a series of fortified villages and hamlets, manned by machine gun crews and dug-in tanks. Once a red flare hissed into the sky some two hundred yards away and illuminated them in its blood-red light. Peters reacted at once. He fired a white flare from the pistol attached to the SP's side, and the flare seemed to satisfy the German sentries.

They rumbled on, guided by Banu who seemed to know every hamlet in the immediate area of Novorossiysk. Just before dawn they were in the outskirts of the port and Crooke realised it was time that they got under cover. In the end, when no convenient wood presented itself in which they could hide during the daylight hours, he decided to take a chance. Some two hundred yards away, outlined against the dirty white of the false dawn, he spotted a lone tumbledown farm and a couple of haystacks. He bent down to Thaelmann who was now driving and roared into his ear: 'Go for the haystack and bury the thing in it!'

Thaelmann nodded and thrust the Ferdinand into bottom gear. The SP crashed through the rickety wooden fence surrounding the farm, and headed straight for the haystack. Over at the single-storey farmhouse the door flew open and yellow light streamed out. Thaelmann did not let himself be deflected. As Peters, Banu and the Yank dropped over the side, he struck the haystack squarely in the middle and cut the motor at the same moment. The stack collapsed on top of them and effectively concealed the SP.

When Crooke finally managed to get the

straw out of his face and pushed his way out of the mess, the other three had already forced their way into the farmhouse, its sole decoration a wooden bench running the whole length of the great tiled oven which took up most of the space. An old woman stood there, her withered toothless face like that of a mummy shrunk by the sun, her ancient rheumatic hands raised in terrified supplication. Next to her stood a small barefoot boy, tears of fear streaming down his dirty face, his skinny arm held protectively around an emaciated moth-eaten ass as if he were prepared to die for it.

Crooke came to an abrupt halt at the low doorway. He was a little ashamed at causing so much fear in these two bundles of rags. Gradually Banu managed to calm the old woman. The little boy dried his tears and stared curiously at the strange intruders. Crooke took out one of the precious sovereigns, and offered it to the old woman, who grabbed it eagerly. She bit it and her eyes almost disappeared into her deep wrinkles. She said something which Banu translated for Crooke.

'It's good,' she explained. 'The woman says we're safe here. There are no Germans for over a kilometre. We can stay.'

Hastily the Destroyers went to work to cover up the traces of their presence. With the help of the boy and the Yank, who had been brought up on a farm, they patched up the mess they had made of the haystack, while Gippo and Stevens repaired the smashed fence. In the meantime Crooke and Banu climbed to the small height above the farm so that he could survey the port down below.

Already the sun was coming up behind them and shooting its first rays across the water. In the port the first thin wisps of smoke started to emerge from the chimneys. Somewhere a donkey began to bray for its feed.

'To your left – away from the beach,' Banu directed his gaze. 'Up the avenue there. Then on to the large square. Do you see it?'

'Yes.'

'Now the white-painted house beyond the square. You can just see the flag waving.'

'Yes, I am with you,' Crooke responded following her instructions.

'That's the Germans' headquarters.'

Crooke stared at the nineteenth-century house guarded by a high white wall which ran right round, broken only by a large gate which he thought (though he wasn't quite sure in the treacherous dawn light) was covered by a sandbagged position. So that was where the Caucasian Fox lived!

'It looks a tough nut to crack – difficult to get into,' he added hastily in case Banu did not understand the English idiom.

'Yes, a very clever people the Germans,' she answered slowly, as if she were talking to herself, 'in some things. But fools in many other ways. You know when they first came here there were those among us who welcomed them. We thought they were coming here as liberators.' She shrugged expressively and threw back a lock of her jet-black hair which had fallen over her forehead. 'But they were too clumsy and in some cases too cruel. A very superior people who had no time for their inferior new subjects.'

Crooke could hardly visualise the Germans as liberators. He took his eyes away from their target and expressed his surprise. 'You welcomed the Germans?'

'Yes. Anything to escape from Stalin. We told ourselves that nothing could be as bad as that.'

'You mean the Circassians?'

'Yes. But we paid for it,' she added dourly.

'How?'

'When the Germans broke off their offensive last year and we knew they couldn't win, the Georgians began to take their revenge. They are a violent people, you know. After all Stalin is a Georgian himself. They started to murder all potential opponents to their own regime. My father included.' Suddenly tears flooded her eyes. Crooke touched her hand hesitantly, but she pulled herself together at once and her face hardened again. 'They crucified him.'

'What!'

'Yes, Loladze did. In 1942 he was a high ranking officer in the NKVD. He had courage enough to stay when the rest of the Russian pack fled Tiflis because they thought the Germans were coming. When the Germans did not come, he took a leaf from the book of his master Beria and indulged in unlimited cruelty.'

'Beria?'

'The head of the NKVD. The most feared man in Russia. A sadist who they say beats naked teenage girls for his filthy sexual tastes. Loladze is just as perverted. He must inflict pain – see people suffer.'

'A sadist?'

'Yes, a sadist who killed my father. Don't

ask me how it happened. All I know is that my people found my father, dead – thank God. Nailed to one of our crosses – we are a God-fearing people – with his eyes out and his tongue … his tongue,' she faltered momentarily, 'cut out and placed on the plate for communion at the foot of the cross.'

Her face twisted in a cynical smile.

'Yes, such a people we are,' she said bitterly, forgetting her excellent English for a moment.

Crooke tried to visualise the scene: an old man nailed to an improvised cross; then the afterthought. The hasty search for a knife. The crude jokes at the old man's dying agony. The bloody piece of flesh being dropped cynically into the silver plate. The old man's hideous mutilated cries as he died and the jeers of the triumphant Georgians below.

Crooke shook his head hard, as if he wished to get rid of the picture by force. He turned to the woman. 'That's why you helped us, isn't it?' he said softly. 'You are really after Loladze?'

'Yes. One day – one day soon, I shall kill him.'

That afternoon they saddled the boy's skinny donkey to the little panje cart and, praying that the animal would be able to last until they got to town, the woman, Crooke, Thaelmann and the boy set off to reconnoitre the port of Novorossiysk.

As they came closer to the town, Crooke told himself that Philby had been right. This was an important headquarters. On both sides crudely painted skull-and-crossbones signs indicated extensive minefields and as they turned into the dirt road, they were faced by a large cemetery with row after row of crude birch crosses decorated with German steel helmets.

'The fighting of last year,' Banu explained softly as a group of barefoot peasant women passed them, bearing bundles of vegetables for the market and urging protesting geese in front of them. 'Many Germans were killed then.'

'And the Russians?' Thaelmann asked.

'They don't need crosses. They are godless.'

They plodded on, submerging themselves in the throng of peasants heading for the market. Slowly they progressed through the low wooden huts of the suburbs into the centre of the port with its shabby stone business houses and villas.

Suddenly Banu whispered, 'Germans.'

Crooke who had tried to adopt the same shuffle as the white-dressed, barefoot peasants all around him faltered momentarily. Fifty yards away two hard-faced German military policemen stood motionless in red and white striped sentry boxes, surveying the Russian crowd with suspicious eyes.

'Chained dogs,' Thaelmann whispered, indicating the silver 'MP' plates around the army policemen's necks. 'That's what the German soldiers call them.'

Crooke absorbed the information, but did not think it wise to say anything at that moment. Instead he allowed himself to be forced by the sullen crowd of Russians past the guards towards the port. But as he moved forward, head downcast in humility, his eye sized up the details of the Caucasian Fox's HQ – the stiff metal army flag, the waiting vehicles in the cobbled yard, the staff officers with the crimson stripe of the general staff down their breeches, puffing a last cigarette before attending some morning conference, the attentive orderlies and all the rest of the comings and goings which indicated a high level headquarters.

Some minutes later they broke away from

the shuffling crowd of peasants and squatted in the dust at the side of the cobbled road which led down to the busy harbour filled with Russian fishing boats and the long grey shapes of German E-boats. A few bored German soldiers in heavy, dusty boots strolled up and down, and twenty yards away a ragged fisherman sat on a rusty bollard and repaired his net. No one took any notice of them.

Crooke nodded to Miron, the little boy. Obediently he took his lean donkey to a patch of grass some dozen yards away and made a great play of urging it to crop the sparse sunbaked vegetation. He was a good lad and understood that he had to warn them if the Germans got too close.

'All right,' Crooke said out of the corner of his mouth, his gaze fixed on the hard earth in apparently dumb peasant fatality. 'Miron and I will check out the port. You, Banu, and Thaelmann go back up the road to his HQ and see what you can find out there. We will meet again here in an hour's time. Understood?'

They nodded and a few moments later split up.

There were six E-boats in the harbour, their decks filled with busy white-clad sailors obviously preparing the flotilla for another mission in the Black Sea. Crooke, squatting on his haunches as he had seen the peasants do in Egypt, surveyed them through half-closed eyes. If the Destroyers could pull off their mission, one of the boats would be the quickest way out of Russia and back to Turkey. But how the devil would they be able to take over one of the fastest German motor launches, especially as not one of the Destroyers knew the slightest thing about boats?

He did not have time to consider the problem at length. A boot thudded into his ribs and an angry voice said, *'davoi – hau ab, mensch!'* A burly German sailor in a little blue peaked cap was staring down at him, rifle slung over his shoulder. Obviously a sentry. Crooke gave his best imitation of a frightened Russian peasant and calling 'Miron' scrambled hastily to his feet. The German aimed another kick at him and missed. He muttered something angrily, but refrained from having another go. Perhaps it was too hot for such exertion. Hurriedly Crooke and the boy got out of his way.

Five minutes later he was back at their meeting place waiting impatiently for the other two. He did not have to wait long.

Pretending to be yet another group of bored Russian peasants, they bent their heads and listened as Banu told them what she had learned: 'Every morning your Fox has conferences with his staff and then he eats punctually at one o'clock. After the Germans have eaten he always leaves for the front.'

Thaelmann took up the story. 'I kept my ears open, sir, to the chatter of the *Landsers* – the German soldiers on the street. He's well liked. The ordinary soldier thinks he's one of the best. Not the usual Prussian aristocrat. After he's eaten, he takes the coastal road. This one. At the edge of town he picks up a couple of armoured cars from the guard company. Apparently he doesn't like it. He hates fuss and bother, but the Führer has ordered he should have an escort because of the danger of attacks by the partisans.'

Carefully Crooke considered the information. Evidently the place to attack the Caucasian Fox was not outside town when he had his armoured car escort, but inside. The question remained *where* inside the town and *how?* Their weapons were limited to Banu's submachine gun and the sten, plus a few odd knives.

'It seems,' he began thoughtfully, 'that the best spot to have a crack at him would be—'

His words were drowned by the roar of car engines. A long, dark-green open Mercedes swept round the corner with a squeal of rubber. A stiff metal army commander's flag decorated the bonnet, but it was not the flag which caught Crooke's eye; it was the face of the man sitting next to the driver behind the set-back windscreen. He recognised it at once from Mallory's briefing; it was that of the Caucasian Fox himself! Crooke and the rest scrambled to their feet. On all sides the peasants were lifting their caps and fur hats in respect. Cheerfully, the Field-Marshal, one big hand resting on his rifle, waved to them as the driver started to accelerate again as he took the coastal road.

Suddenly one of the barefoot, white-kerchiefed peasant women screamed. A precious goose started to waddle across the road in the path of the big car. The driver braked. Too late! A squawk, a wild flapping of wings, a shower of feathers and as the car squealed to a halt the goose lay dead.

The peasant woman flung her apron up to her eyes in horror; her precious goose was gone. She began to howl in despair. The Field-Marshal snapped something to the driver. He called to the peasant woman in Russian. The tears streaming down her wrinkled brown face unheeded, she advanced hesitantly towards the big car. The Caucasian Fox smiled at her encouragingly and taking out his wallet offered her a note.

The woman seized it eagerly. Her tears dried up immediately. Gratefully she grasped the officer's hand and pressed a fervent kiss of appreciation on it. Hastily he drew it back and signalled to the driver to continue. As he passed he touched his cap politely, as if the barefoot peasant were some great Berlin society lady he had chanced to encounter on the Potsdamer Platz. Crooke caught a last glance of his face and then the car vanished in a cloud of dust, heading for the front and the Blue Line.

'So that's your Caucasian Fox,' Banu breathed. 'If all Germans were like that they would have won the war in Russia in 1942.'

Crooke did not comment. He stared at the corner where the peasant woman was busy scraping up the bloody remains of her precious goose from the dust. He snapped out of his reverie and nodded to Miron. 'That's it, Thaelmann,' he said decisively.

'That's what, sir?'

'That corner – that's where we're going to

kill the Caucasian Fox.'

Two hours later, while Crooke discussed his plan with the Destroyers over a humble evening meal and Banu was outside helping Miron to chop wood for the morning, the low door was suddenly thrown open. The Yank dived for the sten. Too late! A bearded civilian, his chest criss-crossed with ammunition bandoliers, stood there, big feet astride, pointing the business end of a submachine gun at them. To his right the window shutter flew open. Another Russian tommy gun barrel poked through it – and another. Slowly the Destroyers started to raise their hands.

Standing at the big oven, the old woman started to cry, repeating the word '*Partizan*' over and over again until the bearded civilian strode over to her purposefully and rammed the butt of his tommy gun into her ancient wrinkled face. Her cries stopped.

The partisan turned to them. With a grunt he crooked a dirty big finger at them '*Davoi,*' he ordered.

They did not understand the word, but they recognised its meaning well enough. 'Move.'

Sullenly they filed outside.

In the fading light they saw that the house was surrounded by dirty scruffy civilians mounted on ponies, all pointing their assorted weapons at the Destroyers. There was no sign of Banu or Miron. Perhaps they had been lucky enough to escape. They, however, were prisoners.

CHAPTER FOUR

The next hour was spent in a hurried progress through dark woods and the edges of huge sunflower fields as they climbed higher and higher into the hills above the port, with their captors urging them on in a mixture of fear and truculence, prodding the Destroyers with their weapons and repeating the words '*davoi, davoi*' whenever they began to lag behind. Then their speed slackened and their captors seemed to relax. The prisoners became aware of cunningly concealed outposts in the dark fir woods. Once they stopped and what was obviously a password was exchanged. They proceeded now at an almost leisurely pace. Five minutes later they were filing through a narrow fissure in the rock wall ahead of them, to emerge into a huge underground cavern, their eyes smarting at the sudden light and their nostrils assailed by the stink of petrol, oil and stale air.

'An underground factory,' Stevens said, as they paused and stared at the cave which was divided up by metal screens, behind which nearly a hundred lathes hummed and rattled, while sweating operators turned out rifle barrels.

'Yes, the partisans often have them,' Thaelmann explained. 'Stalin's order was that they should be self-sufficiently–'

His explanation ended in a grunt of pain as the bearded leader of the partisans poked him in the back and urged him forward. They threaded their way through the lathes, passing through what must have been the kitchen where heavy-set women with cropped hair peeled potatoes, rifles slung over their shoulders; then on to the rear of the cave where a few trestle tables, roughly covered with grey blankets, indicated the underground factory's headquarters. With a rough command and threatening gesture to match, the bearded partisan leader ordered them to stop. Stiffly he marched towards a man standing with his back towards the Destroyers, apparently studying some sort of progress chart attached to the rock wall, and made his report. The other man listened attentively, nodding his head a couple of times, but still not turning round. At last the bearded partisan was finished. He stepped back three paces like a wooden puppet, clicked to attention and waited.

There was no sound save for the whirr of the machines and the chatter of the women in the kitchen.

At last the black-jacketed man at the chart turned round and faced the Destroyers, his handsome face grim and forbidding. For what seemed a long time he did not speak, but examined each of their faces. Finally he poked a thumb at his chest and said throatily '*Ya Loladze.*'

None of the Destroyers spoke Russian, but they understood the gesture well enough, 'I'm Loladze – and I'm proud of it.' Loladze had swept-back grey hair and a clipped iron-grey moustache, typical, Crooke guessed, of the high-ranking NKVD officer he had once been. But his hard black Oriental eyes glittered with peasant cunning, and there was something about the droop of the thick, sensuous underlip that confirmed the woman's statement that Loladze was a sadist.

'Do you speak English?' Crooke asked.

Without waiting for an answer the Yank pushed by the guard standing at his side and thrust his face into Loladze's. 'I thought you Joes were supposed to be our Allies?' he snarled.

Loladze gave a barely perceptible nod to

126

the guard who raised his machine pistol and brought it down hard on the back of the Texan's skull. The Yank groaned softly. His eyes glazed over and he sank to the floor.

'Hey, what the hell's going on?' Stevens cried angrily and stepped forward. A dozen machine pistols were immediately levelled at him.

'*Stand fast!*' Crooke shouted. 'Let me deal with it.'

Crooke turned to the partisan leader once more and repeated his question.

Loladze shook his head and said: '*Ya ne ponimyu.*'

Thaelmann tried him in German.

His answer was an impassive thick '*Nix versteh.*'

Crooke looked at Gippo who before the war had sold pornographic photographs to tourists in Egypt. 'You have a go, Gippo.'

Obediently the half-breed tried, twisting his face into that ingratiating smile which he must have used to advantage with the pot-bellied tourists who streamed ashore from the cruise ships, eager for some safe taste of Egypt's celebrated pre-war low life. Rapidly he went through the whole range of languages known to him until the look on Loladze's face changed and Crooke knew

127

that Gippo had provoked a response.

The half-breed explained. 'I ask him if he understands. The Armenian gentleman would look but would not pay–'

'And ask him if he understands that we are British soldiers. Tell him that we're friends.'

With a great deal of waving of hands and at seemingly interminable length, Gippo tried to put across Crooke's words.

Loladze did not seem to be surprised by the information.

'Doesn't look as if he's going to put out any flags to celebrate the event, does it, sir?' Stevens whispered to Crooke.

'No.'

'Imagine the reaction if a Russian landed at Newcastle or somewhere like that just out of the blue,' the Guardsman said, staring at Loladze's impassive face curiously. 'You can just imagine the fuss the local lads would make. You'd almost think that this bloke knew we were coming.'

'You could be right there,' Crooke said. He turned to Gippo again. 'Try to make it clear that we're friends – allies. With them. We're here to carry out a mission to help Russia. We need their help.'

Gippo did his best with his limited pornography pedlar's knowledge of Armenian.

Finally he achieved a reaction. But it wasn't a pleasant one. Loladze spat suddenly at their feet and then very slowly and deliberately drew his finger across his throat. Suddenly Gippo went very pale beneath his dark skin.

'Yer don't have to tell us what the miserable sod said,' Stevens commented easily, but there was no mistaking the note of fear in his voice. 'We're off for a Burton. Yer don't need to be any bleeding professor to understand that.'

Gippo confirmed Stevens' interpretation. With dry lips he said: 'That's what I am thinking he said, sir.'

Crooke flashed an angry look at the Russian's impassive face. 'Now let's get this straight,' he snapped. 'You want to kill us. Why – we're Allies.' Hastily he grabbed his twin plastic military identification discs and thrust them at the other man. 'Look at these if you don't believe me – I'm a British officer.'

The partisan leader's grim look did not change. Slowly he repeated the words '*Ya ne ponimyu,*' and then, in throaty German, '*Morgen du tot.*'

Then he rapped out something in his own language. A couple of guards dragged the

129

Yank roughly to his feet and hustled him towards the far end of the cave.

It was a long night.

All around the busy underground factory continued to function. When one shift was finished, another group of workers took their places at the lathes while the original operators flung themselves down wearily on the heaps of oil sacks at the back of the cave. Even if the Destroyers had wanted to go to sleep, it would have been impossible. But the Destroyers had no time for sleep, even the Yank whose head was bothering him. Through half-closed eyes they watched their guards closely, hoping that they might drop off as the night progressed. But they were disappointed. The surly heavily-armed partisans who guarded them were changed every two hours as in any regular military establishment and each new group watched their captives with equally hostile eyes.

Stevens nudged Thaelmann and said glumly. 'Nice little playmates you've got.'

'They're no playmates of mine,' was all he had to reply. Even his usual enthusiastic response to everything communist had been stilled by the totally unexpected reaction on the part of the partisans.

Time passed.

The Yank crawled to Crooke, his left hand still holding his injured head protectively. 'If I tried to jump one of the bastards,' he began, 'couldn't you guys–'

Crooke cut him short. 'No use, Yank. Even if we could pull it off, there's probably half a hundred of them out there. No, our only chance is outside. Perhaps we could make a run for it, once we're out of this damned place.'

Stevens yawned loudly. The guards frowned at him. 'Never say die, sir,' he said. 'We'll be laughing at this in a hundred years' time.'

'In a pig's eye!' the Yank snorted.

The mist still hung in the valley below, but it was starting to take on a brassy tint as the pale yellow sun tried to burn through it. To their right, further up the high plateau, the Destroyers could make out a couple of white farm buildings, from which the first straight plumes of blue smoke stood stiffly in the dawn air.

Their bearded captors broke the silence and pushed them back against the rock face. A group of eight young men, tied together by ropes, were making their way awkwardly towards them, urged on by a handful of guards. The prisoners were led by a tall, big-boned, long-faced farmer with long arms and large homely red hands that hung below the sleeves of his ragged fur jacket. It was far too small for him and made him seem more pathetic than he really was.

'*Schpion*,' one of their captors said, and hawking, spat deliberately at the feet of the big-boned farmer as he came level with them. The prisoner did not deign to look at him. Yet, in spite of his pose, it was clear that he was afraid, terribly afraid. Their guards bellowed a series of orders.

Obediently the prisoners shuffled into an awkward line. Hastily a guard ran behind them threading a rope around their wrists and tugging them behind the prisoners' backs. That done, another guard stepped forward and began to pin large white paper circles over each prisoner's heart.

'So the buggers won't miss,' Stevens commented, but the words sounded very strange as if spoken by someone else.

The guards formed a rough line. Obviously they were the firing squad. A few minutes passed in silence. The Destroyers stared over at the prisoners. The tall farmer was moving his lips in silence. Perhaps he was praying.

Loladze, freshly shaven, his face gleaming with health and good food, stepped from the cave. He nodded to the partisan in charge of the firing squad.

The latter rapped out an order. Up in the trees the crows cawed hoarsely and rose lazily into the air, startled by the noise. The partisans raised their rifles. To their right Loladze lit a long Russian cigarette and puffed at it calmly, as if he were in some theatre watching a play and not the final act in eight young men's lives.

The firing squad commander rapped out a further order. The Destroyers could hear the rustle of stocks on the partisans' clothing, as they pressed the butts more firmly into their shoulders. Then came the burst of rifle-fire. The tall farmer stiffened. Behind him bullets chipped the rock wall. He began to sink to his knees. Beside him the other prisoners were galvanised in one last terrible final frenzy as the bullets struck them. Loladze flipped away his cigarette. Without haste he walked over to the men on the ground, drawing his pistol as he did so. Then bending over each body in turn he pulled the trigger. There was a dull muffled explosion. Dead or not, each body jerked under the impact of the bullet. Finally Loladze straightened up, his task finished. Slowly he walked over to the Destroyers, his eyes glistening strangely, as if the task he had just completed had given him great pleasure.

He said something to their guards and stepped back.

The guards pushed them forward roughly.

The same deadly procedure began while slowly, infinitely slowly, the seconds passed. Loladze watched them intently, puffing at another long cigarette. Suddenly the silence was broken by a steady drone of aircraft from the south. The Destroyers looked upwards. The partisans, too, paused in the midst of their preparations and looked to the sky.

A large black V-formation of slow-moving three-engined aircraft was roaring ever closer.

'Junkers 52,' Peters said, licking dry lips. 'Tell them anywhere.'

A guard stepped forward over the bodies of the men shot before them and started pinning crudely-shaped white paper circles on their chests, while behind him the firing squad formed up again.

'What do you say, Guardsman,' Stevens tried to joke. 'Them lads wouldn't make the Brigade, would they?'

Peters tried to smile. 'The Grenadiers might take 'em – they'd take anything. But not the Coldstreams. After all the Grenadiers'd take anything that was warm and could blanco a belt.'

Crooke felt a sense of pride in his men. German, American, half-breed, English – the Destroyers were facing the inevitable end in the way he had always known they would ever since he had taken them out of Cairo Military Prison: bravely, without quavering. The Destroyers were going to live up to their reputation to the last.

Now the Junkers 52 formation was directly above them at about six hundred feet, obviously on their way to bomb Tiflis or Baku in preparation for the new German offensive. The man in charge of the firing squad opened his mouth to shout the final command which would put paid to the Destroyers for good, but decided to wait until the deafening roar of the German planes was gone. Then bright green flares suddenly soared into the air from all sides, coming from the woods below them. There was the clatter of tank tracks. Up above them scores of bodies hurtled from the low-flying Junkers. Moments later bright white parachutes broke open. The sky was filled with them. Ragged small arms fire rattled out of the trees. A guard clasped his shoulder and sank to his knees.

'*Nmetski!*' Loladze shouted. He swung round and started firing at the dark figures emerging from the trees.

In an instant all was chaos and confusion, firing coming from all sides, with parachutist after parachutist hitting the dirt a couple of hundred yards away and expertly freeing themselves from their billowing silk chutes before flinging themselves into the nearest cover to join in the attack.

The partisans had been taken by complete surprise. While the Destroyers kneeled as best they could behind the bodies of the dead 'spies,' the German paras in their baggy overalls and rimless helmets advanced, supported by the infantry, brought up in half-tracks and tanks.

Within a matter of minutes it was all over. First one and then another of the Russian partisans threw down his gun and raised his hands in surrender. The handful grew into a dozen and then a score. Soon it was a mass surrender, the partisans tossing aside their rifles and tommy guns and, kicking aside their dead and wounded, streaming towards the German paras, hands clasped over their heads, crying *'kamerad, kamerad'* over and over again in their haste to get out of the firing line.

Slowly the firing died away. At the mouth of the cave a couple of the heavy-set, cropped-haired women they had seen in the kitchen continued to fire until a young para officer in a camouflaged jacket, the bright black and silver of the Knight's Cross flashing at his neck, mowed them down with his Schmeisser. It was over and the paras started to collect the prisoners.

For a while no one seemed concerned with the Destroyers roped together in the middle of the battlefield, the crude white circles still stuck to their chests. But at length, as Loladze, blood trickling from a wound in his forehead, was thrust into the circle of partisans who stood there trembling, hands clasped over their shaven skulls, the young officer with the Knight's Cross came across to them.

Surprisingly he bowed slightly, as if he were being introduced to them at some social occasion and not in the middle of a bloody battlefield. 'May I introduce myself,' he said in good but guttural English. 'My name is von Foelkersam – Baron von Foelkersam of the Brandenburg Regiment.'

He looked directly at Crooke. 'You are Lieutenant Crooke, no doubt.'

'No, sodding Doctor Livingstone!' Stevens growled, but there was no denying the relief in his voice.

'How do you know?' Crooke asked.

The young officer pushed back his rimless helmet and wiped the sweat from his brow. He grinned. 'My chief, Admiral Canaris, has some good sources of information in London. You would be surprised, Lieutenant Crooke, what we do know about you – *and your Destroyers!*' He emphasised the last words, as if to heighten the surprise.

Crooke did his best to live up to the young officer's expectations; he could well guess where Foelkersam's information came from. 'But how did you know we were here?'

Foelkersam waved his hand at the woman emerging from the nearest half-track. It was Banu!

'The good *Fraulein Doktor* was kind enough to tell us what had happened to you.' He grinned like a mischievous schoolboy and wagged a finger at them. 'And we could not afford to lose the valuable Destroyers to the likes of that communist swine over there.' He nodded at a sullen Loladze, who was still holding his bleeding head.

'I see,' Crooke said and watched as the Circassian woman slowly walked towards them, clutching something tightly to her bosom. She came level with them. 'Banu,' he said softly.

She did not reply. Her eyes were fixed on Loladze. It was as if there were no one else present but the partisan leader and herself.

'*Banu,*' Crooke said sharply.

Still no reaction. Slowly she lowered her hand from her bosom. Glass gleamed in the thin light of the morning. Loladze became aware of her presence. She was only a matter of yards away now. He opened his mouth as if to protest.

Foelkersam saw her intention. '*Halten Sie das Weib!*' he screamed, but he was too late. Before anyone could stop her, her hand shot out and the contents of the bottle flew in Loladze's face. He staggered back screaming, his hands clapped to his face. Blindly he stumbled to the side of the nearest half-track and slithered down it, writhing and yelling in agony.

Von Foelkersam sprang forward. He knocked the mesmerised woman to one side and the bottle dropped from her fingers. He bent down and turned Loladze's face to the light. The acid was everywhere. Already it had eaten deeply into the once-handsome flesh. Drops of it were still dripping from the man's hair and burning their way into his ears. One eye was already a white opaque glaze, as if someone had spat into it. The other was beginning to go. In a matter of moments he would be completely blind.

The young officer rapped out a series of orders. A soldier unclipped the Red Cross box from the side of the half-track and dropped it over the side. But it was too late. Loladze's face had disappeared like that of a painting with which the artist had been disappointed and had removed with one stroke of his wet sponge.

For a moment the horrified medic attempted to remove the acid with a cloth while Loladze moaned pitifully. Finally he rose stiffly and shook his head. He muttered something to the officer.

Von Foelkersam bit his lip. '*Der Gnaden-schuss?*' he said half-aloud. 'The *coup de grace.*'

The medic shrugged. Slowly, while the Destroyers watched as if hypnotised, he drew his pistol and with difficulty placed it at the base of the writhing man's skull. He hesitated. Then he pulled the trigger. There was a muffled explosion. Loladze's body arched, then sank back. The partisan leader was dead.

Six yards away Banu crossed herself hastily, suddenly snapping out of her trance. 'God forgive me,' she cried in her own language. Next moment she fainted.

SECTION THREE:
THE ESCAPE

'The price of your freedom is the assassination of Mr Winston Churchill.'

Baron von Foelkersam, Regiment Brandenburg, to the Destroyers

CHAPTER ONE

'*Ach, die Herren Englander,*' the Caucasian Fox greeted them as they were led into the big, sun-dappled dining room by Baron von Foelkersam, where the staff of the German 20th Army sat eating at long scrubbed wooden tables. He rose, sweeping out a big hand expansively, said to his staff in English, 'These are the gentlemen from England whom you have heard so much about from our friends in London.'

The assembled staff officers paused in the middle of eating and stared at the ragged Destroyers standing sullenly in their midst under the guard of a cautious von Foelkersam, a drawn pistol in his hand.

The Caucasian Fox grinned. 'Please forgive our stares, gentlemen. But we lead a quiet life down here with our little war. You are some excitement for us.'

'Yeah buddy,' the Yank snarled *sotto voce*, 'you'll get ya excitement one day, don't you worry.'

The Field-Marshal did not seem to hear

145

the remark. He waved his hand to Foelker-sam. '*Mein lieber Herr Baron,* please put away your pistol. I have heard that the Destroyers are fierce. But I think that this day we have drawn their teeth, yes?' Without waiting for von Foelkersam to reply, he raised his voice and bellowed '*Ordonnanz!*'

The door flew open and a white-coated soldier clicked his heels, his hands pressed rigidly down the sides of his grey trousers. The German snapped something at him and then, turning to the Destroyers, said: 'But please take a seat at the table over there and join us in our food. It is not much – pea soup and *Wurst.* What do you call it in America – one of you is from the United States, yes?' He stared along their ranks. 'A hot dog, I believe?' Obviously the Field-Marshal was proud of his knowledge of English.

'Yeah and you'll get a hot foot from me,' the Yank said thickly, as they were escorted to the empty table by von Foelkersam.

Moments later the white-coated orderly placed a bowl of thick green soup before each one of them. They had not eaten for twenty-four hours and, forgetting their surround-ings, attacked the food with a will while the Germans continued their own meal, occa-sionally glancing over at the hungry

146

Destroyers and making whispered comments to themselves.

Their hunger finally appeased, they dropped their spoons and stared as the orderly was now handing out cigars to the staff officers. He hesitated at the Destroyers' table, but the Field-Marshal indicated with a nod that they should be given one too. 'Now, gentlemen,' he said, puffing at his cigar, 'before we begin I think a schnapps would be in order.' He turned to the orderly. *'Schick' das Frauenzimmer 'rein.'*

The door opened and Banu stood there with a tray of glasses in her hands.

Peters' face fell.

'Look at that damned bitch,' Stevens said angrily. 'She sold us to the Jerries to get her own back on that Loladze.'

'I should have taken her knickers off back at the village,' Gippo said, 'then things might have been different.'

'Knock it off,' the Yank snapped. 'I wouldn't touch a lousy two-timing broad like that – even with yours!'

Swiftly with downcast eyes she passed along the tables, placing glasses in front of the assembled officers. She hesitated when she came to the Destroyers' table. 'Yes, the Englishmen too,' the Field-Marshal ordered, noticing her hesitancy. 'And let us hope the schnapps will not be so potent as the other liquid you used.'

The Caucasian Fox raised his glass until it was parallel with the third button of his jacket.

'Typical Prussian drinking style,' Thaelmann whispered as the Destroyers watched all the other officers do the same. 'When he gives the command they'll all drink together.'

'*Prosit, meine Herren!*' the Caucasian Fox rapped.

'*Prosit, Herr Generalfeldmarschall!*' the assembled officers cried as one and like a lot of robots raised their glasses mechanically and drained their fiery contents in one gulp.

The Caucasian Fox put down his glass firmly on the wooden table and nodded to von Foelkersam. The young officer picked the bundle off the floor at his feet and placed it in front of the Field-Marshal. 'Gentlemen,' he addressed the Destroyers who were still sipping schnapps, 'may I have your attention.'

Swiftly he unwrapped the bundle to reveal a brand new sten gun. Holding it so that the assembled officers could see it, he said; 'A simple weapon, gentlemen. In our money I should say it would cost–' he shrugged –

'perhaps twenty reichsmark to produce. It has already been demonstrated to the Führer. But the Führer in his wisdom has decided that the Tommies could never produce a weapon better than anything already in the possession of the glorious Greater German Army.'

There was a ripple of laughter among the assembled officers and Crooke had the feeling that the Field-Marshal was no friend of the Führer.

For a moment there was silence while the Fox turned the weapon over and examined it with professional interest. When he looked at the Destroyers again his face was hard and serious. 'I am surprised, gentlemen, that you are so generous with such an excellent weapon.'

'What do you mean, sir?' Crooke asked.

The Caucasian Fox looked at him directly with narrow eyes. 'Baron von Foelkersam's men found ten containers of them in the cave inhabited by your late friend Loladze.'

'Bloody hell, that's ripe – our friend Loladze!' Peters snorted.

'Shut up,' Stevens hissed hastily. 'Of course he thinks we were in cahoots with the Russki.'

'Jesus, with friends like that,' the Yank

added, 'we don't need enemies!'

The Caucasian Fox noted their constern-
ation, but misinterpreted it. 'Yes, I am sure
you are surprised that your friends did not
take better care of such excellent machine
pistols. But you do not understand the
Russian mentality like we do.' He paused
and his face grew serious again. Leaning
forward over the scrubbed trestle table, he
said, 'Don't you Tommies realise that you
are digging your own graves by helping
those Red bandits?'

Thaelmann opened his mouth to protest
but the Field-Marshal waved him to silence.

'Do you think they will stop if they ever
break through the German Army? First it
will be Poland, then the Balkans. Germany
and Western Europe will go next. France,
Belgium, Holland – the Channel coast.' He
looked along their dirty, sullen faces as if he
hoped to find something there which
corresponded to his own sense of urgency.
'Then it will be England itself with your Mr
Churchill hanging in his own Ten Downing
Street.'

Stevens laughed hollowly. 'The Russians
might be a funny lot of beggars, General,' he
said boldly, 'but they are our Allies. Go on,'
he jeered, 'pull the other leg – it's got bells

on it!'

'Shut up!' Crooke snapped.

But the Cockney's words had had their effect. The urgency went out of the Field Marshal's face. He sighed wearily. 'You are right perhaps. There is nothing more foolish than this war which will mean the end of both our countries – and the British Empire.' Slowly he pushed back his chair and rose to his feet.

As one man, the assembled staff officers sprang to attention. The Field-Marshal placed his cap on his cropped blond head and picked up his rifle. '*Meine Herren!*' he snapped, '*ich empfehle mich.*' Touching the peak of his cap to acknowledge their salutes, he strode out of the big dining-room; it was time to go on his daily inspection of the front line.

Two hours later Baron von Foelkersam was ushered into their cell. For a moment he stared in distaste at the dirty, straw-covered floor, with the rusty evil-smelling latrine bucket in the corner. The aristocratic young officer had shaved and changed into a clean summer uniform, complete with all his decorations. He gave off a faint odour of expensive cologne. Stevens nudged Gippo.

151

'Oh kiss me, for I'm to be Queen of the May!' But there was no enthusiasm in his voice; the Destroyers' spirits had slumped at finding themselves once again in jail after such a narrow escape from death.

The German nodded to the MP guard. Obediently he closed the door behind von Foelkersam. Patiently the latter waited until it was locked, then he stepped into the centre of the room, his nose wrinkling slightly as he passed the stinking bucket. He pulled a piece of paper from the cuff of his white jacket. 'Let me read you something,' he said unfolding it. 'It is part of the Führer Commando Order of 18 October 1942 in my own translation.'

Without waiting for their reaction he started: 'I therefore order, from now on all enemies on so-called commando missions in Europe or Africa challenged by German troops, even if they are to all appearances soldiers in uniform or demolition troops, whether armed or unarmed, in battle or in flight, are to be slaughtered to the last man. It does not make any difference whether they are landed from ships and aircraft for their actions, or whether they are dropped by parachute. Even if these individuals, when found, should apparently be prepared to give themselves up, no pardon is to be granted them on principle. Any imprisonment under military guard in POW camps for instance, etc., is strictly forbidden, even if this is only intended for a short time.'

He paused and looked at their tense faces, before continuing: 'I will hold responsible under Military Law for failing to carry out this order, all commanders and officers who either have neglected their duty in instructing the troops about this order or acted against this order when it was to be executed.' He allowed the words to sink in, then added: 'You see, gentlemen, my hands are tied. I can do nothing to help you.'

'What do you mean?' Crooke asked, though he already knew the answer to his own question.

'You are commandos. You are in civilian clothes behind the German lines. You understand the consequences.'

The Yank gave a mock groan of dismay. 'Jesus, we're not for the chop again, are we?'

'If you mean by that, this' – Foelkersam made the gesture of clicking a trigger against his temple – 'yes.'

'First the Russkies and now you guys, everyone wants to give us the order of the purple shaft!'

For a moment there was silence. From

outside came the steady tramp of the sentries and the permanent dry rustle of the locusts in the sunbaked courtyard.

'However,' the Baron broke the silence, 'I have informed my chief, Admiral Canaris of the *Abwehr,* of your capture. He, in his turn, has notified the Führer and the Führer has agreed to the Admiral's plan.'

'And that is?' Crooke said drily, carefully avoiding any sign of the new hope that had welled up within him.

The Baron toyed momentarily with his Knight's Cross. 'Gentlemen, let me say first that Admiral Canaris is an honourable man. We are in the fourth year of a total war, but he still attempts to observe the international code of military conduct, in spite of the pressures placed upon him from certain quarters. For instance, he resisted the attempts to have a certain important French general in our captivity shot while trying to escape. And there were others like him who Admiral Canaris has protected in spite of Party pressure. Shot while trying to escape.' He looked carefully at Crooke. 'You understand?'

Crooke did. It was a favourite trick of the Gestapo to get rid of undesirables whom they couldn't legally murder, by having them 'shot while trying to escape,' as the cynical formula had it.

'But things are changing in our circles,' the Baron continued. 'Last year there was El Alamein and Stalingrad,' he shrugged in the Continental manner, as if this were explanation enough. 'The times now are desperate and they require desperate measures. Soon I too will be leaving the *Abwehr* and joining Skorzeny of the *Friedensthaler*. My new chief is working closely with the Admiral, but his are the methods of 1943, not those of 1939.'

Crooke breathed out a deep sigh. The Destroyers, in spite of their desperate situation, grinned. They knew how hard it was for the CO to keep his temper when anyone couldn't get to the point. 'But, Baron,' he said patiently, 'what has all this got to do with us?'

'All right then, Mr Crooke, let me put my cards on the table. Will you work for us?'

The Destroyers looked at the young German officer, mouths open in amazement.

'How?' Crooke asked.

'You could – er – escape, with our assistance.'

'And then?'

'You could get back to London and report that your mission was unsuccessful.'

'And then?' Crooke persisted. 'There must

be a catch.'

Foelkersam hesitated momentarily. 'You could do a job for us.'

Crooke laughed. It was not a pleasant sound. 'Why should we do anything for you – once we are safely back in London? What pressure could you exert on us there?'

The Baron nodded at Thaelmann. 'We'd keep your tame Red. That would be our hold upon you.'

Thaelmann, the former German communist who had escaped from Dachau and had sworn he would never go back into a concentration camp, paled; but he said nothing.

'All right,' Crooke snapped. 'What's all this rigmarole about? What do you want us to do? What is the real price of our freedom?'

Foelkersam fingered his Knight's Cross. 'If – let us assume – you could escape with our aid and get back to your own country, who would you report to?'

'Our chief – Commander Mallory of Naval Intelligence, as you well know from your much vaunted sources in London.'

'And then?'

'To the Chief of Naval Intelligence perhaps,' Crooke replied, wondering where the German's questions were leading.

'Anyone else?' Foelkerswam persisted.

'C – head of British Intelligence perhaps – I'm sure I'm not betraying any state secrets,' Crooke added cynically. 'It's quite obvious that you know about him too.'

'No one else?'

'Now look here,' Crooke threatened to explode.

Baron von Foelkersam waved him to be calm. 'Please be patient with me, Lieutenant Crooke,' he urged. 'After all it's your lives that are at stake. *Please!*' The young officer seemed genuinely concerned. He considered a moment.

'Well, after we got back from Africa, the PM – Mr Churchill – received us.'

The serious look disappeared from the young German's face. 'That's what we thought.'

'What do you mean?'

'I mean – please let me say once again that we live in times that demand desperate if unpleasant measures. Well, gentlemen, the price of your freedom is *the assassination of Mr Winston Churchill!*'

CHAPTER TWO

'That stupid kraut must be nuts!' the Yank exploded after the Baron had departed, leaving them with the bombshell effect of his suggestion. 'Jesus, I'm not a guy who goes much on Churchill. I know guys in my hometown who'd sooner plug Roosevelt than shake his hand. But I never did hear so much crap in all my goddamn life. *Kill Churchill, I ask ya!*'

'The Jerries must be barmy – off their rockers,' the Guardsman joined in when Crooke did not respond.

'I'm agreeing,' Gippo echoed, 'off their rocking horses undoubtedly. Killing Mr Churchill – how can he expect us British fellows to do something like that!'

Crooke let them talk. For what seemed a long time he was sunk in a moody silence, staring thoughtfully at Thaelmann who did not join in the chatter of the rest. Outside the sentries plodded back and forth.

Suddenly he broke his silence. 'Well, I for one,' he said in an unnaturally loud voice, 'don't think the Baron's suggestion is a bad idea, as long as we can ensure nothing happens to Thaelmann.'

Stevens, who was just in the middle of a long diatribe against 'them bloody stupid Huns', broke off and stared at his CO in bewilderment.

'After all,' Crooke continued, rising to his feet and staring down at them aggressively, 'what has the British state ever done for us? We're generally regarded as the scum of the British Army, aren't we! Look at Gippo here – kindly jailed because some fool of a rear echelon doctor couldn't look after his wife or his money. Or you Yank, sentenced to the gashouse because you thought you were doing right, killing men who attempted to kill you right to the last moment and then thought they could escape by raising their hands in surrender! All of you – every single one of you – has suffered because of your bravery in the British cause.'

There was a deathly silence in the grim little bug-ridden cell. They stared up at their pale-faced, one-eyed CO as if he were completely mad.

Crooke poked a finger at his own chest. 'And what about me? I lose my eye and in spite of possessing the country's highest decoration, I'm demoted with my career in the Regular Army in ruins. Why? Simply because I wanted to fight and not sit on my bottom in some damned office in Whitehall. That's why,' he added bitterly.

He paused for breath while Stevens gaped at Gippo aghast. In a strained voice he whispered. 'It's all been too much for him – these last few days. The poor bastard's gone doolali!' Peters rose to his feet and went over to the water bucket. He dipped in the ladle and offered it to Crooke. 'Would you like a drink of water, sir?' he asked solicitously.

Crooke dashed the ladle to the ground. It fell with a clatter. 'Take your damned water,' he snarled, but a grin was beginning to light up his face.

'Oh my God,' Stevens breathed, 'he's gone complete bonkers now.'

But Crooke was not crazy. Hastily he said in the bastard Arabic that they all knew from their years 'up the blue,' as they called the Western Desert, '*Entebaa … b'surra.* If they are listening let them think they are right. We are prepared to work for them.'

The Yank opened his mouth to say something and Stevens gagged him quickly. 'You think they have a microphone hidden in the

160

cell somewhere?' Gippo asked in Arabic.

Crooke nodded hastily.

'*Effendim,*' Gippo clapped his skinny brown hands together in delight at Crooke's cunning. It was worthy of an Arab.

'Yes,' Crooke continued in the bastard language. 'We must co-operate. Understood? And now sleep, *M'sael Kheir.*'

'*M'sael kheir, Hawaga Crooke,*' they chanted solemnly and relaxed on their lousy straw pallets.

If the Baron were still listening at his hidden mike, he heard no more that night save the heavy snoring of six utterly exhausted men, trying to regain their strength for whatever the morrow might bring.

Crooke's Destroyers had learned a lot from their months in Cairo Military Prison. As they plodded steadily around the little exercise yard, with the sun gleaming brightly off the white-washed walls, under the watchful eyes of the MP guards six feet above them, they appeared silent, almost sullen. But unknown to the guards who could not see their lips, a stream of messages was passing back and forth, gabbled from the sides of their mouths.

'Listen,' Crooke hissed, 'to agree with the

161

Baron is our only way out of here – alive. We must listen carefully to his plan and look for the loopholes. A way to turn it to our own advantage. The Jerries are no fools. They'll know our people in Istanbul will check up on us as soon as we get back. We'll be vetted. Okay, so the Germans'll have to fake an escape for us.'

The little procession stopped abruptly as Stevens picked up one of the guard's cigarette ends and puffed it into life again. Crooke took the opportunity to hiss, 'That faked escape might give us the freedom of action we need to do the job we came here to carry out.'

'And me, sir?' Thaelmann asked.

Crooke had no time to answer his question. On the wall the sweating, ill-tempered sergeant in charge of the MPs bellowed, '*Los … weitermarschieren!*' The big hand clasped on the machine pistol slung across his heavy chest lent emphasis to his order.

They plodded on.

It was later that same day that Baron von Foelkersam came to their cell once again. After circumventing the evil-smelling bucket, which no amount of lime helped, he got down to business at once. 'Gentlemen, may I ask if you are prepared to go ahead

162

with our little plan?'

'We've discussed it,' Crooke said slowly, 'and we have come to the conclusion that it is the only way out as far as we are concerned.'

'Good,' the Baron said enthusiastically and his relief was obvious.

'There is only one condition.'

'And that is?'

'Thaelmann comes with us. You know as well as we do that once we return, our security people will start checking up.'

The Baron nodded his understanding.

'Well, how could we explain Thaelmann's absence?' Crooke queried. 'You don't know how our security people operate. They are hard and efficient and they'd seize upon that part of a cover story and tear it apart.'

The Baron tugged at the decoration dangling at his throat. 'A very good point, Lieutenant Crooke. However, we have prepared for that eventuality. Let me explain the cover story we have thought out for you. Undoubtedly if your superiors have any contact with the Red — which from those sten containers it is obvious they have — they will know by now that you are our prisoners. They will expect too that you will shortly — er—' he hesitated. Evidently Baron von

Foelkersam was a very fastidious man and not only about his appearance. 'Be executed, if you'll forgive me. Naturally they would be surprised if you turned up therefore in their midst, just like that.' He spread out his hands, palms upwards. 'You understand?'

The Destroyers nodded but said nothing.

'*Also,* we must make it appear that you attempted your mission and failed it *logically*. Thereafter – and I emphasise this – you escaped *equally logically*.'

He looked at them as if he expected them to make some comment. Again they remained silent.

'In a couple of days' time the Field-Marshal will be making an inspection tour of the coast south of here by boat. You can probably guess why. It is part of the preparations for our summer offensive. More details you do not need to know. All I can tell you is that it will smash the Reds for good.'

'Like Stalingrad?' Thaelmann asked.

The Baron ignored the question. 'You will accompany the Field-Marshal on this tour. Your cover will be that he wanted to see the spot where you landed. You will tell your authorities that you thought he was interested in the place on account of his own plans – something or other like that. Well, during this voyage when you attempt to kill the Field Marshal – in theory only, naturally, you will follow up your failure by a successful escape to your friends in the hills. Yes, your former friend, the woman Banu, has told us all about them. She has been most helpful. Undoubtedly once you have contacted her Circassians, they will help you across the border. They are very reliable people with no love for the Reds, the woman has assured me – and very good cooks,' he added jovially. 'The Field-Marshal has taken a liking to the woman's cooking in fact and she is now on his staff.' He emphasised the words for some reason. 'Once in Turkey, you will contact your people at the embassy and go ahead with the mission as planned.'

'And providing we can get away with this crazy plan,' Crooke snorted, 'what happens to us then?'

Von Foelkersam shrugged. 'That is a chance that you will have to take. I have, however, been in communication with the admiral and he tells me that if you are successful and could get to somewhere remote – say like Scotland – the *Kriegsmarine* might risk a seaplane from Norway to get you out.'

'Generous of yer,' Stevens commented dourly.

'As you English say,' the Baron summed up their situation, 'you are between the devil and the deep blue sea.'

'It's our only chance,' Crooke said as they stomped around the exercise yard the next morning. 'There is nothing we can do in here. Everything depends on that boat. Anyone know anything about boats?'

As they circled the yard under the watchful eyes of the 'chained dogs,' they all shook their heads slightly to indicate that they didn't.

'A fine bunch of dogsbodies you are,' Stevens commented. 'That dirty nignog behind me even gets seasick when he washes himself, which ain't often – I can tell yer!'

Suddenly their whispered conversation was silenced by Thaelmann's urgent 'Banu!'

The big Circassian woman stood in the door of her kitchen, her sleeves rolled up, a bowl of washing-up water in her hands.

'Christ, she don't even have the shame to blush,' Stevens complained. 'Look at her – you'd think butter wouldn't melt in her sodding mouth.'

As they came level with her, Gippo's dark eyes took on an evil, malicious look. Licking his lips lecherously he stuck up his thin,

166

brown middle finger offensively. 'Now, woman,' he called, 'sit on that!'

She flushed. Suddenly she spat expertly in the dust at their feet. With a violent sweep of her brawny arm she flung the bowl's filthy contents at them. Gippo ducked and its contents caught the surprised Peters full in the face.

Swiftly she turned. But before she closed the door behind her, she flung up her skirts at the back to reveal a quick glimpse of soft white rounded naked flesh. It was the ultimate female gesture of contempt.

On the wall the 'chained dogs' roared with laughter and approval. Even the dour MP sergeant's face lit up. Thus neither he nor the rest spotted Crooke picking up the kitchen knife with a note wrapped around its handle which she had flung at them with the washing up water.

'Read,' Crooke said swiftly in Arabic, once he had finished it in the protection of their cell, passing it on to Stevens. 'Take your time – then we destroy.'

While the slip of wet paper passed from hand to hand, he mulled over the woman's pencilled message once more. In her neat, typically academic, writing, she had written:

'Forgive me. It was the only way for me to have my revenge on Loladze. I hope you will understand? Now I can help you. The German General will leave here in two days in the E-boat *Moewe*. You will go with him. I too, as cook. I am in contact with my people here in the town. They have given me something to help you. When the time comes, trust me. Your friend, Banu.'

The Guardsman was the last to read the note. It seemed to take him longer than the rest. 'Hurry up,' Crooke said in bastard Arabic, 'in case the Baron comes.'

The Guardsman, still wet from the washing-up water, slipped it hastily into his mouth and began chewing on it.

Stevens grinned. 'Now that's what I call real love – greater love hath no man,' he said cynically, happy at the Guardsman's embarrassment.

The latter flushed even more. Unable to speak, he raised his fingers and gave Stevens the soldier's version of the famous V-sign introduced by Churchill.

But Crooke did not notice the badinage; his mind was too full of the possibilities opened by the woman's note. What did she mean – 'they have given me something to help you'? What could it be – weapons? His brain raced with new hope and the manifold possibilities now beginning to emerge. *Operation Caucasian Fox* might not fail after all.

CHAPTER THREE

The roar of the E-boat's diesels stopped abruptly. On the open bridge above them the young skipper rapped out an order. The *Moewe's* knifelike bow which had been cleaving the water at forty miles an hour started to fall. Slowly the 92-ton E-boat slid through the Black Sea to a halt.

The Field-Marshal smiled gratefully. Turning to the handful of staff officers and the Destroyers, who had been holding on to any support they could find for the last hour, he said, 'Not exactly the best way to prepare oneself for food, gentlemen, is it? My stomach feels as if it has been in a cocktail shaker for the last hour.'

The staff officers and von Foelkersam, who had come along as their conducting officer, laughed dutifully.

As the *Moewe* came to a stop, the Caucasian Fox turned his attention to the deserted shore, rippling in the late afternoon heat, while behind them the destroyer, *Elbe,* which was their escort, dropped anchor in the deeper water. For a while the Field-Marshal studied the coast, then he dropped his binoculars and turned to the others. 'After Stalingrad and our tremendous losses of last year,' he explained, obviously more for the Destroyers' benefit than that of his staff, 'our Supreme Command was faced with a great dilemma. Should we stand on the defensive for instance? Or should we undertake a limited offensive against the Reds?'

He paused and smiled a little cynically and Crooke could see why his men admired the Caucasian Fox so much. 'The gentlemen in Berlin naturally think we should attack. In Berlin it is easy to think like that. As a result Colonel-General Model will attack in the north and in the south Colonel-General Hoth will do the same with his Fourth Panzer Army. To carry out their attack with the necessary force in a great pincer operation, they will require *all* our reserves.'

He sighed, and for a moment stared glumly at the shore some five hundred yards away.

'My task, gentlemen, will be to stand fast here. Fortunately the ground favours the defensive. As you can see,' he turned to Crooke, as if it were quite natural that a humble lieutenant should have the situation explained to him, 'it is mainly mountains broken up by rivers. In addition there are large corn and sunflower fields, which make visibility poor. Hence it is not good tank country, you understand?'

Crooke nodded, while the rest of the Destroyers listened attentively to this strange German officer who treated them more like comrades than the prisoners they were.

'Naturally it is not tank-proof, as some of the gentlemen in Berlin would like to believe. Fortunately I have my old veterans holding the Blue Line. They will make up for any failings in the equipment in the 20th Army.' He grinned suddenly, as the young skipper came down from the bridge and joined them. 'We here have an old joke about my veterans. We say that when – and if – the great victory parade takes place in Berlin, the populace will cheer the be-medalled Field-Marshals marching through the Brandenburg Gate in front of their victorious young heroes. And so the parade will go on until finally in the rear one of my ancient corporals will appear, laden down with all his weapons and bearded to the waist. When they ask him why *he* is there, he'll reply in Russian '*Nix ponimyu*'. He will have been so long in Russia that he has forgotten to speak German!'

Crooke smiled politely. There was no denying the Field-Marshal's pride in his battered command. He took a last look at the shore. 'Now, Baron, are your killers well enough briefed on the German plans for their people back in London?'

Baron von Foelkersam, as elegant as ever in spite of his sea sickness, clicked his heels together. '*Jawohl Herr General-feldmarschall.* Quite sufficient for the Tommies back in London.'

'Thank you.' He turned to the skipper. 'We shall eat in a few minutes, Captain,' he explained, 'and afterwards we shall get under way again. I want to be back in my headquarters before midnight.'

'Yes, sir.' He saluted smartly and marched off back to the bridge.

The Field-Marshal smiled and said, 'And now, gentlemen, I suggest we all go and eat before you carry out your assassination attempt and make your escape.' He looked at Crooke. 'I hope you are all good swimmers.'

Crooke nodded, but said nothing, not trusting himself to speak. This was it. Time was running out rapidly, and they still had no idea of how Banu intended to help them.

The Field-Marshal turned and headed for the E-boat's small wardroom. Baron von Foelkersam indicated that they should follow. Thaelmann looked at Crooke unhappily. The officer pressed his arm firmly. 'Don't worry,' he whispered, 'we're not going without you.'

While the Germans and their prisoners took their places at two separate tables in the cramped wardroom, as the E-boat rocked gently on the swell, Crooke could see that it would soon be dark; the rays which streamed through the ports were coming in at an acute angle. At the most they had another hour, for it was von Foelkersam's plan to drop them over the side as soon as the sun went down, so that only the *Moewe's* crew knew of the deception.

His mind racing, yet fully aware that everything depended upon Banu, Crooke tried to relax. Moodily he stared at the little wardroom with the sun sparkling on the silver and white table-cloths. The scene in the cabin might well have been taken from a pre-war P&O prospectus advertising a cruise 'to exotic climes.' The parallel was heightened by the large smiles and appreciative 'ahs' of the Germans, as the *Moewe's* two white-jacketed stewards entered bearing large bowls of *borsch*. Swiftly the cold, dark-red Russian soup was served and then it was the Destroyers' turn. The rating who acted as a steward plonked the white bowl on their table, spilling a little of its contents and growled in German: 'Help yourselves.'

But if the temporary steward was surly, the Caucasian Fox was friendliness itself. He raised his glass of sparkling red Crimean wine and toasted them with *'Hals und Beinbruch, meine Herren.'*

'Happy landings,' Thaelmann interpreted for Crooke's benefit, as he toyed morosely with his soup.

Then the Field-Marshal noticed they had nothing to drink and tinkled the bell on the table in front of him. The surly steward appeared at the door. 'Something to drink for my guests,' he ordered.

'The Russian woman,' he meant Banu obviously, 'says there is only one more bottle of wine for you, sir. There is beer–'

'Then let them have beer.'

A few moments later Banu herself appeared in the doorway, a tray with glasses and beer bottles held under her bosom. *'Pivo,'* she said stupidly and looked blankly at the Field-Marshal.

'The English,' he said in Russian. Banu took off the first bottle cap and poured the beer into Crooke's glass. It frothed over and ran down to the tablecloth. She placed the bottle on the table noisily and grunted '*Davoi,* get on with it.'

When she had gone, Crooke, with his back to the Germans' table, toyed idly with the bottle, pretending to be studying the green label, covered in an unintelligible cyrillic script. Intently he listened to the Germans eating; they were still occupied with the excellent cold soup. Flashing a warning glance at the Destroyers who had seen the slip of white paper attached to the base of the bottle too, he pulled it off and read it:

'Do not touch wine. Drugged. Be alert.'

He gave the others a brief nod and thrust the note in his mouth, washing it down with a drink of beer. So that was her plan. Happily he tackled his soup.

The meal dragged on interminably. The famous Circassian chicken was brought in to the accompaniment of 'ahs and 'ohs' on the part of the German staff officers. The first bottle of champagne was finally emptied to be replaced by another. It disappeared more slowly. Still no sign that its contents were having any effect. Anxiously Crooke kept casting covert glances over his shoulder. It was not until the surly steward brought in the *Baklava* that it was clear the drug was beginning to work.

The Germans' faces became flushed. Their movements began to be unusually slow, as if they were in an advanced state of drunkenness. Once von Foelkersam dropped a spoon and instead of waiting for the steward to replace it, he groped for it clumsily himself and nearly fell from his chair. The steward shook his head. He was disgusted; the big wheels were getting drunk again. He left the wardroom.

With unconcealed fascination the Destroyers watched as a fat, flushed Colonel, the Field-Marshal's chief-of-staff, slowly but inevitably pushed back his glass and slumped head first on to the table, setting the plates trembling.

The Field-Marshal's mouth fell open, as if he were about to explode at this breach of etiquette. But then his lips slackened and his mouth sagged stupidly. Slowly his big hand, bearing his glass, drooped. The glass dropped from his nerveless fingers and shattered on the floor. No one at the Germans' table seemed to notice it. Abruptly he keeled over and slipped to the floor.

The Destroyers hesitated no longer. Crooke sprang to his feet. 'Check the door, Gippo,' he ordered. He bent down and whipped the pistol from the chief-of-staff's holster and flung it to the half-breed. Gippo caught it, while von Foelkersam watched them in paralysed horror.

Then he too began to fall over. Even before he hit the table, the Yank had dashed across and pulled out his pistol.

'All right, lads,' Crooke ordered softly, throwing a quick glance at the *Elbe* riding on the gentle swell in the dusk. 'Stevens, you stand by the door with Gippo. I'm going to call the stewards.'

'Right, sir.' Stevens joined his mate at the other side of the door.

Crooke rang the bell.

The first steward – the surly one – entered. For one moment he stood there and stared at the drugged officers open-mouthed.

'This is going to hurt you more than me, chum,' Stevens said gleefully and hit him over the back of the head with an empty champagne bottle.

A few moments later the second steward suffered the same fate and joyfully Banu burst in on them and gleefully hugged them with unrestrained exuberance.

Crooke let the Destroyers have their moment of triumph, but only a moment; time was of the essence. 'Banu,' he broke into their wild exchanges of news and explanations, 'how many crew has the ship?'

'Twenty-one,' she said, 'I counted exactly this morning.'

'And where are they now exactly.'

'They all eat from the same kitchen—'

'Galley,' Stevens interrupted. 'You ain't much of a sailor.'

'The captain has already eaten, he's on the bridge. The engine crew are at their stations ready to sail. The rest, perhaps fifteen men, are eating in their quarters.'

'Good,' Crooke said, 'couldn't be better. One last question: how far do you think we are from the Turkish frontier now?'

She thought a moment. 'Perhaps four hundred kilometres.'

'I see,' he considered for a moment. 'It's a long way, but we might manage it. We'll try at all events to get as much mileage out of this ship as possible.'

'What do you mean, sir?' Peters asked, standing happily near the vindicated Banu.

'We're going take over the *Moewe*.'

'But sir,' Stevens protested, 'that destroyer

out there could knock the stuffing out of us with its first salvo.'

'Agreed, but you mustn't forget that we've got one advantage – we've got the Field-Marshal as a hostage.'

They followed the direction of his gaze.

'The *Elbe* wouldn't fire on us with him aboard – not for a while at least until they have checked with higher headquarters. The problem is to get the *Moewe* underway.' He turned to the American. 'Yank, get up on the bridge as casually as you can with Thaelmann.' He indicated the machine pistol which the American had found in the stewards' quarters. 'Hide that thing under your jacket. Once you're up there, Thaelmann, get the skipper to head for the nearest Turkish port.'

'And if he won't, sir,' Thaelmann said simply.

'I'll take care of that one, Thaelmann... The bridge is connected to the wardroom by the speaking tube. Tell him that he can verify with me, if he doesn't believe you – but we'll kill the first German officer within one minute of his refusing to obey the order. And we'll work our way up until we've got only the Field-Marshal left.'

The Yank grinned. This was rapid action

after his own killer's heart. 'Will do, chief,' he said happily.

'All right, on your way.' He addressed himself to Gippo and Stevens: 'Take it nice and easy and work your way along the rear deck until you get to that 20mm twin ack-ack gun. My guess is that once the boat gets underway, somebody from the crew will come up topside to have a look at what's going on.'

'So the first one that comes up for a shufti,' Stevens interrupted, already ahead of his CO, 'gets lead poisoning sort of sudden.'

Crooke nodded. 'That's right. Or at least make war-like noises so that the crew keeps below decks and out of our way.'

'Right, sir.' Stevens turned to Gippo. 'Come on yer filthy nignog. Get yer nasty wog eyes off the lady's knockers and let's be at 'em.'

With the two of them gone, Crooke spoke to Peters. 'I'm relying on you to watch them,' he indicated the drugged German officers. 'With a bit of luck and a lot of praying we might just pull this thing off after all.'

Peters, happy that Banu was safe and that she had managed to help them in such a spectacular manner, grinned. 'I'm pointing my prayer rug towards Mecca already, sir.'

Five minutes later there was a shrill whistle from the tube. Crooke sprang up to it. A babble of excited German struck his ear. '*Moment,*' he cried out, after whistling up the tube and trying to stop the German skipper. '*Moment.*'

The flow of words about the two 'crazy Tommies' died away. 'Listen, Captain,' he said carefully in English, 'I've got the Field-Marshal down here. If you don't start the engines in one minute and get underway as you have been ordered, something unpleasant will happen to him.'

For a moment there was no response from the bridge. Crooke could sense the young German's mind racing as he considered his course of action.

'You have thirty seconds left,' Crooke said icily. 'Make up your mind quickly.'

'*Scheisserkerl* – damn you!' the skipper cursed. Suddenly the tube went dead and Crooke knew he had won. 'Watch them,' he snapped at Peters. 'I'm going up top.'

Crooke clattered up the metal steps. Below him the ship's engines grunted and burst into life. The boat shook.

Topside the deck was empty save for the two grinning Destroyers poised at the 20mm gun. Crooke waved. He ran towards the bridge. The young skipper was issuing a stream of orders to the engine room, prodded on enthusiastically by a happy Yank, while Thaelmann listened tensely to the German in case he tried to trick them.

Crooke threw an anxious glance at the *Elbe,* silhouetted against the setting sun. The scene was a perfect picture of peace and calm: one, however, which, as Crooke knew, would be rudely disturbed once the *Moewe* got underway.

Suddenly the E-boat's diesels burst into full life. The skipper bellowed something to the engine room crew. He pushed the controls to full power. The E-boat shot forward, its roar destroying the evening peace. Its nose began to tilt. It hit the first new wave with a solid bump, as if it had struck a wall. Crooke staggered and turned to stare at the *Elbe.* Still no movement. He braced himself, legs apart, as the *Moewe* shuddered below him.

There was a shout. A member of the crew popped his head out of their quarters. Stevens pressed the button of the twin 20mm. A stream of white tracer spat from the gun and the sailor screamed and fell back clutching his bleeding face. But Crooke had no eyes for him. His gaze was fixed on the silent destroyer which was rapidly falling away behind them. How long would it take for them to react?

Then a white light began flickering at the destroyer's bridge. On and off in rapid succession. An Aldiss lamp.

'Skipper,' he called to the German captain above the roar of the diesels. 'What are they saying?'

'I cannot see through my back,' he muttered in thick guttural English.

'You heard the CO,' the Yank snarled and dug the muzzle of his machine pistol hard into the German's back. 'Talk!'

The skipper looked over his shoulder, trying to balance himself against the tilting motion of the *Moewe*. 'What … has … happened?' he read out the signals. 'Why … are you moving… Please report my–'

He never finished.

Below, Stevens, caught in the wild euphoria of the escape and the speeding boat, acted without orders. He swung the 20mm round. A burst of tracer hissed across the waves. The light went out, shattered by the Cockney's first burst. But even in the midst of the excited cheers that went up from the deck below, Crooke could hear the roar as the destroyer's engines burst into life. The *Elbe* had taken up the chase.

CHAPTER FOUR

The *Elbe* caught up with them two hours later. In spite of all the young skipper's efforts, urged on by the Yank's machine pistol, they were not able to out-distance the more powerful destroyer. Slowly the gap between the two ships was cut down steadily until one hour later the lean destroyer was sailing almost parallel with the *Moewe*.

A searchlight flicked on, groped its way through the darkness until it finally rested on the *Moewe's* bridge, blinding the men standing, legs braced against the violent vibrations of the E-boat's engines going full out.

Crooke sheltered his eyes against the silver glare. 'Yank,' he ordered, 'knock the bloody thing out.'

'With the greatest of pleasure,' the Texan said.

Balancing himself against the edge of the open bridge, the American aimed carefully. The Schmeister's maximum range was only about 150 yards, but the Yank was a crack shot. Suddenly he squeezed the trigger. There was the sharp crackle of lead. A vicious stream of red flame shot out of the machine pistol's muzzle and the searchlight went out. For ten full minutes nothing happened while the destroyer came closer and closer to the E-boat. Now the men on the bridge could see its bulk quite clearly and make out the sharp outlines of its crew standing along the railings.

Suddenly a loud-hailer cut in above the roar of the engines. A metallic impersonal voice cried something in German.

'What did he say, Thaelmann?'

'We must surrender – we have no chance. If we do not stop they will blow us out of the water.' Thaelmann indicated the destroyer's four 5-inch guns swinging round threateningly in their direction.

Crooke seized the E-boat's loud-hailer and thrust it into Thaelmann's hands. 'Tell them,' he roared, 'that we have the Field-Marshal in our hands. Any offensive action on their part would risk the Field-Marshal's life.'

Thaelmann carried out Crooke's instructions.

Expectantly Crooke waited for a reply when his voice died away. But none came.

The threat had had its effect, though the one-eyed officer knew it would not be long before the captain of the *Elbe* received his instructions from Dönitz and he could guess what those might be.

Thus the two German ships sailed side by side at top speed through the night, with every precious hour that passed taking the escapees closer and closer to the Turkish border and freedom.

Dawn broke with the startling suddenness of the East. But it was not the fiery red ball of sun which abruptly popped over the horizon that woke Crooke from his uneasy doze on the bridge; it was the crack of the *Elbe's* twin 5-inches in the forward turret and the harsh orange flash which penetrated his closed eyelids.

Three hundred yards away the destroyer shuddered violently. A suddenly wide awake Crooke could see the dark objects tumbling their way awkwardly through the velvet dawn sky twenty odd yards away.

The little E-boat rocked from side to side. Icy water roared over the side and soaked the men on the bridge. Crooke gasped with the impact. Crazily bent against the motor boat's violent swing to port, Crooke ran over to Thaelmann. 'Get the skipper.' He indicated the German holding grimly on to the controls, seawater pouring down his pale, tense face. 'Get him to take evasive action.' He bent his head over the edge of the bridge and roared to Gippo and Stevens: 'Fire, fire.'

His words were drowned by the rapid chatter of the 20mms. Shell cases began to clatter noisily to the ship's heaving deck.

'Yank,' he yelled above the roar, 'get up to that 37mm cannon! It's not much. But see what you can do!'

The American needed no second invitation. He doubled away while the young skipper flung the E-boat from side to side, knowing that his own life was at stake too now; the *Elbe's* shells were not making any distinction between friend and foe.

Crooke knew now that the *Elbe* would not hesitate to sink the *Moewe* even if it meant killing the Field-Marshal. Obviously her captain had consulted the highest authorities and had been told that the Field-Marshal, who knew the full details of the great summer offensive, must not be allowed to fall into enemy hands. The *Elbe's* next salvo confirmed he was right. A shell struck the

Moewe towards the bow. A sudden gap appeared in the metal. A hoist twisted like molten glass and dropped overboard with a great splash. Deck plates reeled upwards grotesquely, and as jet black smoke shot up from below decks, hot shrapnel hissed through the air. Crooke ducked hastily. Suddenly Stevens and Gippo appeared through the smoke coughing thickly, tears streaming down their faces.

'Where's Yank?' he cried above the noise.

'Here,' the American answered, appearing behind the other two, 'the bastards got the 37 before I could get to it.'

Crooke patted him on the shoulder. 'Okay, Yank, get up on the bridge and man the machine guns – it's the best we've got left. You, Stevens, nip down below and tell Peters and the woman to bring up the Field-Marshal. And give the Baron and the rest a dig if they're still sleeping.'

'I understand, sir,' Stevens yelled as he doubled away. 'We've got to give the poor buggers a chance.'

'Never give a sucker a chance!' Yank cried defiantly, enjoying every minute of the action.

Crooke ran back to the bridge. The skipper was still swinging the E-boat from side to side as best he could but the engine room had been damaged and the power was fast diminishing. He was in no doubts about the seriousness of the *Elbe's* gunners. But Crooke had no time for him. 'Yank,' he roared, 'do what you can with those damn guns!'

The Yank bit his lip. 'Okay, get ready to feed the sonuvabitch,' he cried to a tense Gippo holding the long belt of gleaming cartridges. Next instant he pressed the trigger. A hail of lead swept over the water and started pattering against the gun turret's sides. The Yank – a deadly shot as usual – was right on target. Now, his face tense with effort, he tried to work his fore on to the turret's slits in the hope that a lucky slug might penetrate and strike the gun layer.

Beside him Thaelmann, aware that he no longer needed to watch the young skipper, sprayed the destroyer's deck with bullets from the Schmeisser. A sailor clapped his hand to his shoulder and fell heavily. Another threw up both hands in agony and disappeared overboard. Hastily the remainder scattered for cover. Swiftly Thaelmann swung up the blazing machine pistol and started peppering the destroyer's bridge. Whether he was doing any good or not, Crooke could not ascertain, but both boats were heeling wildly as they struck the waves at full speed.

The Field-Marshal staggered up on the bridge groggily, supported by Peters and Banu. The remainder followed him from below, but collapsed on the swaying deck gasping for air.

The *Elbe's* guns roared again. A violent explosion erupted behind them. The men on the bridge ducked instinctively. A shower of metal splinters like spray from a heavy sea swept the whole length of the *Moewe*. The deck became a slippery red mess of dead and dying. The fat chief-of-staff dropped overboard, his blood staining the white foam red for a brief instant before his body vanished.

'*Herrje! Heaven, arse and thread!'* the young skipper cursed when the smoke cleared and he saw the carnage. 'My poor lads! They're butchering them!'

But Crooke had no ears for the skipper's cry of despair. Desperately he cast around for some way out of the trap they found themselves in. Time was running out, he knew that. The *Elbe* was beginning to close in for the kill.

Her twin 5-inch guns fired again. The shells tore the air apart with a sound like thick canvas being ripped. Both struck the E-boat. The *Moewe* shuddered violently and her speed decreased even more. A ready-use locker caught fire suddenly. Ammunition started to explode, sending white and red tracer zig-zagging crazily into the sky. A star shell exploded in the midst of the mad firework display, bathing their faces blood-red. The captain of the *Elbe* was obviously trying to ascertain the extent of the damage inflicted by his big guns. Crooke seized the opportunity offered by a few moment's respite. He grabbed the Captain's arm and yelled urgently, 'Hit the beach!'

The young skipper, his eyes wide with terror, did not seem to understand. 'Thaelmann,' Crooke yelled above the roar of the exploding trace, 'tell him to hit the beach! *QUICK!*'

Without a moment's hesitation, Thaelmann lowered his Schmeisser. He stepped over the debris in the middle of the little bridge and hit the German captain hard across the face. 'The beach,' he roared above the noise. 'Head for the beach, man!' The skipper blinked his eyes rapidly several times, 'Yes,' he gasped, as if he had just run a long race. 'The beach – hit the beach. Only chance.'

193

With all his strength he swung the stricken *Moewe* round in a clumsy half circle. It was difficult, Crooke could see that. But the boat responded.

On the bridge of the *Elbe*, the destroyer's captain must have guessed the E-boat's intention almost at once. He swung the destroyer round in a tight curve at top speed that sent the ship heeling crazily to one side. In the next instant the *Elbe's* forward guns fired again.

Water shot high into the air on both sides. The *Moewe* presented a smaller target now, Crooke told himself. The guns fired once more. The shells exploded a handful of yards in front of them. The men on the bridge ducked as water and metal thrashed over them. Crooke knew the *Elbe's* gunners were bracketing them. If they didn't reach the coast soon, they'd be hit.

Below, the deck was in a state of indescribable confusion. Panic-stricken German sailors were already beginning to leap over the sides, while their wounded comrades dragged themselves pitifully to any cover they could find in the bloody shambles. Another shell hit the *Moewe*, exploding in a shrieking black plume of smoke, a cherry-red flicker at its vicious heart. The *Moewe* almost keeled over. What was left of its shattered superstructure even touched the waves.

Crooke realised that the end was almost there now. 'You help Peters to look after Banu and the German, Thaelmann,' he cupped his hands over his mouth and yelled above the noise and the crackle of the flames. 'Yank, get off that gun! It's no good now... We're finished.'

'Hell, give me another chance at the bastards,' the American snarled, his face coal-black.

Crooke did not argue. He reached up and pulled the Yank out of the firing seat. 'Get going! Stevens and Gippo!' he roared, 'get ready to go when we hit the beach!'

'Yer don't have to ask me twice, sir,' Stevens yelled. He hurried to the shattered twisted railing followed by Gippo, clutching a black metal box, which could well have been the ship's safe.

Now all of them tensed for the shock of impact. The *Elbe* pumped shell after shell at them, but the distance between the two ships was growing again, and Crooke realised that the *Elbe* couldn't come in any further. The water was too shallow. At the controls the young skipper, blood streaming from a wound in his temple, bit his lip grimly as he headed for the beach. The front of the E-boat was obscured by flames now through which they could see dark silhouettes fighting their way to safety.

Suddenly there was a great crash. The front of the *Moewe* folded up like a banana skin and the men on the bridge fell in a heap. For one moment they lay there winded, and there was silence save for the vicious crackle of the flames. The *Elbe* had stopped firing.

Crooke shook his head and staggered to his feet. The *Moewe* had come to rest on what looked like a sand bar. The shore was still fifty yards away. He knew he must act fast before the *Elbe* started lowering boats with boarding parties. 'Come on,' he yelled, 'let's get over the side and out of here – quick!'

CHAPTER FIVE

Weaving from side to side, the survivors staggered through the shallow water, filled with the debris of the *Moewe*, now burning fiercely on the sandbar, its screws out of the water and its white swastika naval ensign hanging limply at its bow.

Crooke reached the shore first. For a moment he stood there, swaying slightly, his breath coming in short sharp gasps with the effort. The *Elbe* had started to move again. Cautiously it was nosing its way through the survivors of the *Moewe,* who, smothered in oil, were shouting and yelling at their fellow sailors lining the destroyer's rails.

He breathed out a sigh of relief. The *Elbe* hove to again. Whether it was to rescue the survivors or whether the captain was afraid to go any further for fear of running aground, he did not know or care. All he knew was that the pause gave him and his men a few minutes respite. He clapped his hands to his mouth and shouted to his men: 'Over here, rally over here, the Destroyers!'

His men changed direction and waded towards him. Peters was first ashore. Still holding his pistol in the Field-Marshal's back, he was helping Banu with his free hand. They clambered up the wet shingle, gasping and spluttering. Moments later the rest of the Destroyers clutching whatever they had been able to save, followed them. 'My goodness,' Gippo said, 'that water is being very cold.'

'Go on,' Stevens said scornfully, bending down to his knees to regain his breath, 'it did yer good, yer dirty nignog! You're clean, at least for a bit.'

Crooke grinned. Nothing seemed able to get the Destroyers down. They had only a matter of minutes before the *Elbe's* captain would come looking for them, once he learned from the *Moewe's* young skipper or von Foelkersam, who had both survived the wreck, that the Caucasian Fox was still alive.

'Cut the cackle,' he ordered. 'Look around and see what you can find in the way of food and weapons.'

'Sir,' Gippo responded, always eager for loot. Hastily, black box tucked under his arm, the water squelching in his boots, he was off to the debris-littered shore. The rest followed. Crooke took a quick look at the Field-Marshal. He was standing quietly, viewing the scene with detached professional interest, almost as if he were watching some training scheme at a battle school and not the real thing at all. Somehow or other he had lost his upper clothing and he was shivering after his exposure to the cold water.

Crooke ran to the water's edge and fished out a blue naval oilskin which he spotted among the litter on the shore. He also picked up a tin which he recognised from the desert as containing black German pumpernickel bread, which would last for months in the can. He ran back to the Field-Marshal and thrust the damp oilskin at him.

'Here, sir,' he said, 'put that on.'

The Field-Marshal's face broke into a smile for the first time since he had come out of his drugged sleep to realise that he was a prisoner.

'Thank you, Mr Crooke,' he said and slipped into it. 'That is very–' His words were drowned by a great explosion. A blast wave, hot and clammy, struck them. Crooke spun round. The *Moewe's* fuel tanks must have gone up. The little E-boat disappeared in a sheet of bright orange flame accompanied by thick oily black smoke which climbed in a straight pillar to the sky.

When the flame died down, the *Moewe* had gone. But Crooke saw that the *Elbe* was beginning to lower her boats. He tossed the tin of bread to Banu. 'Come on,' he yelled, 'let's go. The Jerries are coming!'

Grabbing what they could, the Destroyers began to hurry up the incline of the beach towards the cover of the stunted pines, bent by the winds of the coast, which lay some hundred yards away. Behind them they could hear the steady putt-putt of the *Elbe's* motor launches.

The German marines chased them most of that day as they scrambled along the rugged coast, darting from cover to cover, heading in the general direction of the south and Turkey. Banu's aid was invaluable. Twice they would have bumped into what appeared to be fortified villages, manned by a company of Russian irregulars, if she had not spotted the earthbrown primitive coastal settlements.

For a while Crooke kept a watchful eye on the Fox. But he had apparently resigned himself to his captivity; perhaps the fact that the *Elbe* had sunk the *Moewe* had convinced him his life meant little to the Führer – he was better dead. At all events he kept up with them and made no attempt to delay their progress in spite of the fact that he was a good ten years older than any of the Destroyers.

Towards late afternoon, as they began to force their way through marshy coastal flats, Crooke decided that the Germans had given up the chase. By now they were some fifteen miles from the scene of the sea battle and he reasoned that the *Elbe's* captain would not dare to risk his marines or his stationary ship much longer. After all, the destroyer was anchored in Russian waters. He ordered his panting men to slacken their pace over the treacherous ground, where as soon as they lifted their feet, their footprints filled up rapidly with brackish water.

In the end as the sun began to sink once more on the horizon, he said drily. 'All right, lads, let's take five.'

'*Ten*,' Stevens croaked.

Crooke forced a weary grin. 'All right, ten.'

Gratefully they slumped down on the whitened roots of long dead trees which stood up above the stinking marshy ground, their breath coming in harsh gasps like that of asthmatic old men. For a full five minutes

201

Crooke let them rest in peace, then he wiped the sweat off his brow and said, 'Let's hear what we've got in the way of supplies and weapons, Yank?'

'No chow, but I've got this.' As if it were some great treasure he produced the Schmeisser which Thaelmann had dropped from inside his jacket. 'And I've got an extra mag.'

'Good.' He turned to Thaelmann. 'You?'

He shook his head dourly. 'Nothing.'

He looked at Peters and nodded at the pistol. 'You, Stevens and Gippo, you're our quartermasters – what have you got?'

'A bit of a mess, sir, that's what I've got,' Stevens answered. 'Like they used to sing in the old song. "I've got jam-jam mixed up with the ham in the quartermaster's stores." He dug into his jacket and produced in rapid succession a German salami, with a large bite dug out of one side, a small jar of Russian olives, a packet of ship's biscuits and a small flare pistol. 'Loaded,' he explained, 'and dry.'

'And what about you, Gippo? What's in that box you've got down your jacket?'

Gippo shrugged expressively in the Arab fashion. 'Nothing, sir, nothing at all, sir,' he said unconvincingly. 'But I have this.' He dug in his pockets and pulled out five small round dark tins. 'Chocolate, sir, special German naval chocolate. They are giving it to the Hun sailors so that they can make plenty jig-jig.' He gave a quick visual demonstration of what he meant by 'jig-jig' by shooting back his stiffened lower arm rapidly and thrusting it forward again several times.

Crooke took one of the tins from Gippo and saw that it contained U-boat chocolate. 'Good. Full of vitamins and something to keep the crews awake on long watches.' He tossed it back to Gippo. 'Look after it well. We'll probably need it before we're out of this one.'

'And what about me?' It was the Fox, a faint smile on his broad East German face.

'You?' Crooke said somewhat incredulously.

'Naturally. Am I not of the party?' The Field-Marshal dug into the pocket of the oilskin he had thrown on the ground beside him. 'Perhaps this is something that we can partake of now?' He fetched out an unlabelled bottle. 'Rum,' he said simply.

Passing it over to Stevens for the first drink, the Fox said, 'Give your thanks to the German Navy, Mr Crooke.'

Banu had just taken a drink and was

handing the bottle back to the Field-Marshal, when the seaplane came in low right over their heads, catching the happy little group relaxing in the middle of the marsh completely by surprise. It zoomed down at 20 mph, not more than 350 feet from the ground. Their startled eyes caught a quick glimpse of the dark blob of the pilot in the sparkling glass of the cockpit and the outline of the observer in the Perspex 'blister.' Then the ugly twin-engined seaplane was winging its way out to sea again with its news, hurrying to the *Elbe* which had dispatched it on this reconnaissance mission.

Crooke rose to his feet and stared at the plane, growing ever smaller on the horizon. 'God, what a fool I am!' He swung round on the Fox and, forgetting all military courtesy, he said, 'what happened to those paras who dropped on Loladze's HQ?'

'They went back to their HQ near Berlin,' he answered, without showing any offence at the absence of the normal 'sir.'

'I see. All right, it looks as if they're going to risk sending seaborne troops after us, if they've got no paras. So.' He shrugged. 'We've got to get away from the coast, got to get as deep inland as we can – quickly!' His voice rose. 'All of you – on your feet. We've no time to waste. That seaplane will be back at the *Elbe* in a matter of minutes.'

Hastily they staggered to their feet and started collecting their pathetic little bits and pieces of kit.

'There's just one thing, Mr Crooke,' Banu's authoritative, almost masculine, voice cut into their preparations. 'Do not think that I am afraid,' she said firmly, 'but I must warn you of one thing if we go deeper inland. At this time of the year the dry season has already begun. Ten or twelve kilometres further inland and we shall encounter territory which is little better than desert.'

'So?' he said, busy with his hurried preparations for departure. 'The answer is very simple – we have no water and will have no chance of obtaining any out there.'

Crooke looked at their faces as they stopped in the middle of their packing and stared at him enquiringly. He hesitated a moment. 'That's a chance we've got to take,' he snapped brusquely. 'Come on.'

Without waiting to see their reaction, he turned and began to plod through the marshy ground towards the east. In that direction dark scudding clouds started to obscure the horizon threateningly.

CHAPTER SIX

Just after dawn they emerged from the lush vegetation of the coastal section and rested for a few moments to watch the sunrise. Far away in the east a sharp blade of red cut the white light of the false dawn. For a moment it was still cold from the damp night air. Then abruptly it was hot and the sun was a hanging blood-red ball over the shimmering blue horizon. Crooke indicated the sandy plain ahead stretching as far as the eye could see to the dim outline of the mountains, which marked Russia's border with Turkey. 'All right,' he said, putting his first step on the hard dry sand, 'let's get on with it.'

The march began, with Crooke and the Field-Marshal in the lead and Stevens trailing just behind them. The hours passed. The heat grew in intensity. Their pace started to lag. The Field-Marshal, his lips cracked and scummed, drew off his naval slicker and said thickly, 'the human being, Mr Crooke, consists of seventy percent liquid – fifty litres of it in most of us. If he loses ten litres of that liquid, he dies. I feel I am not far off those ten litres.'

Crooke forced a smile. 'If I may say so, sir, you look in better shape than the lot of us put together.'

'Thank you, but I must say that I don't feel it. However, there is plenty of water here, if one knows how to find it.'

With that he stopped and the column came to a halt behind him. Banu slumped to the ground and Peters slipped off his blouse and hung it over the back of her head to protect her from the sun. Crooke realised that they would have to have a break; they couldn't go on much longer. The sun was reaching the zenith and the heat was terrific. He crouched down on his haunches. 'Where's this water then?' he asked wearily.

'Down there.' The Fox pointed at his feet, and, dropping on his knees, he began digging in the sand, stopping every now and again to clench a handful in his fist, obviously – so Crooke guessed – to check whether it would form a ball. Finally he succeeded. 'You see,' he said triumphantly, holding out his big hand to display the firm, slightly dark sand. 'There's liquid here somewhere. The desert is seldom dry – completely dry. Underground there are streams running for hundreds of kilo-metres.'

'You're right there,' Crooke agreed, remembering his own experiences in the Western Desert prior to the war.

'But how does that help us?' Thaelmann asked, still cautious of the aristocratic German officer, who he obviously regarded as a 'reactionary' and a typical represen-tative of the class which had brought about Germany's downfall. 'We're still not drink-ing.'

'We dig for it simply. But it will take time. So rest and when you are finished you will have water.'

While the Destroyers slumped on the ground watching through eyes narrowed against the white glare, the Fox began to dig until he had reached a depth of a couple of feet. Still there was no sign of water. But the absence did not seem to worry the German. He started to extend the hole. That done, he spread the oilskin over the hole very carefully, anchoring it with the stones that lay around in plenty. Finally, he inserted one of their cans in the hole under the centre of the oilskin and placed a stone on the coat above it so that it sagged directly above the can. That done, he sighed and stretched out in the sand. A few moments later he was snoring gently, hands crossed over his big chest in complete contentment. One by one the Destroyers drifted off as well but Crooke forced himself to keep awake just in case of trouble.

Suddenly he stared up in alarm and blinked his eyes several times. He had fallen asleep. But it wasn't that fact which alarmed him. It was the strange sound. For a moment he could not identify it. Then he recognised the drip-drip of liquid. 'Field-Marshal,' he cried. Like the old soldier he was, the German was awake at once. 'The water, it's there!'

The Destroyers joined him as he crouched over the hole and gingerly removed the oilskin. 'In the heat of the day,' he explained, 'the water under the sand condenses on the rubber inside the coat and then drips into the can – the quantity depends on the area of the coat.' He stepped back. In the centre of the hole, the little can was half-filled with slightly opaque water. Proudly the German lifted it from the depression and handed it courteously to Banu. 'I think you should have the first drink – perhaps two mouthfuls.'

Later that day when their thirst became almost unbearable once again, the ever-resourceful German showed them yet another trick. Ordering Banu to move away, he proceeded to remove his grey-green Army trousers. Then, his shirt-tail flapping a little in the evening wind which was starting to blow up, he tied up the left leg of his pants, while they stared at him as if he were crazy. Then he began to scoop up sand and pack it in the tied-up leg. Satisfied at last with his work, he urinated in the sand-filled leg which he had poised over his empty jackboot, the Destroyers staring at him in open-mouthed amazement.

He chuckled at them. 'You think I am mad,' he said. 'But you will see.'

He was right. An hour later his urine, cleansed of its impurities, began to filter from the sand and into the empty jackboot with a steady drip-drip of clear odourless liquid. When he was satisfied that everything was through he held the boot up to the Yank. 'Would you like a drink my friend?'

Hastily the Yank shook his head. 'Christ on a crutch!' he breathed in utter disbelief, 'wouldya believe it? I never thought I'd see the day when I saw a real four-star general piss in his boot!'

Five minutes later the rest of the Destroyers were minus their pants, spread over the darkening plateau, trying out the same trick.

'Where did you learn all these tricks, sir?' Crooke asked that night as they lay side by side in the cooling sand staring up at the sky.

The Fox chuckled, but there was an element of underlying sadness in the sound. 'I was with the 1932 German expedition to climb Everest. Needless to say – it failed.' He lay on his back, his hands clasped under his blond head, staring up at the stars. 'But it was the happiest time of my life – a time out of life, the confused, chaotic Germany in the throes of the depression. When we arrived back in 1933, Germany was a completely different world.'

Crooke ventured a guess. 'I have a feeling, sir,' he said hesitantly, 'that somehow or other you are glad to get away from your command?'

'In a way, I am,' he turned and, resting his head on his left hand, stared at Crooke. 'Please don't misunderstand me, I am a patriotic German, who believes in his Fatherland. I swore an oath of loyalty to the

Führer and when we went to war with Poland in 1939 I did my duty. I felt the war was in the best interest of my country. After all, soldiers only get real promotion in wartime, as you undoubtedly know.'

'Yes.'

'But,' his voice was suddenly serious again, 'the war has dragged on for four years now. Many of our best men have fallen. But we are no further on the road to victory than we were in 1939. Stalingrad and El Alamein were turning points in my thinking, Crooke. Any realistic soldier, however loyal and patriotic, must realise that we cannot win now. If we are to save what is left of Germany from being overrun by the Red hordes Germany must end the war.'

Crooke propped his head up on one elbow and looked at him. 'But would your Führer agree to that, sir?'

The Fox shook his head slowly. 'Naturally not, Mr Crooke. But then the Adolf Hitlers of this world can be removed, can't they?' It was then that Crooke felt a load lifted from him. He knew abruptly that the Fox could live – *would have to live* – if this war were to be brought to a speedy conclusion. For the first time since they had abducted him and he had begun to plague himself with the awful thought that soon they would have to kill him on Mr Churchill's express order, he felt a sense of relief.

Somehow or other the German must have instinctively realised what had been going through his mind. 'So you see, Mr Crooke, you will have no further problems with me, will you?'

'No, sir.' Crooke responded avidly.

Somewhere a long way off a wild animal began to howl. It was an eerie sound, yet it gave Crooke a new feeling of confidence; for it was the first sign that there was other life than themselves in the dreary waste. Suddenly he felt very tired. 'Well, sir, I think I'll try to get some sleep now. Good night, sir.'

'Good night, Crooke.' For an instant he felt the Field-Marshal's firm hand on his shoulder reassuringly. Then it was gone. Moments later he was asleep.

CHAPTER SEVEN

The Messerschmitts came in at dawn. Zooming in low at 450 mph, they caught the Destroyers and their companions in the open, the pine forests at the foot of the snow-capped mountains still a couple of miles away. At once their machine guns began to crackle viciously.

Lead stitched a deadly pattern in the sand all around them. With an ear-splitting roar that made them duck instinctively, they flashed over the Destroyers' heads at one hundred feet. Next instant they were winging high into the sky, preparatory to their new attack. Crooke, his ears still deafened by the roar, reacted immediately. Cursing himself for not having expected this form of attack – obviously the Me's had been launched from the merchant ship on the Black Sea, the old British convoy protection technique – he yelled, 'Scatter! For Christ's sake! And run for the woods! It's our only chance!'

They needed no urging. Spreading out

hastily on the bare plain that offered no cover whatsoever, they began to run, their anxious eyes fixed on the sky.

This time the two Messerschmitt 109s, their yellow spinners standing out against their stark black bodies, came out of the sun. It was an old fighter pilot trick, calculated to blind their opponents. Before them their shadows flew over the floor of the plain like great black harbingers of death.

Crooke, running beside the Fox, his mouth wide open, gasping for breath, cried tensely 'When ... I shout drop ... *drop* immediately!'

The roar of their motors grew ever louder. Crooke could see the heat waves rippling over their snouts quite clearly now. Suddenly the lead plane lurched and seemed to stop in mid-air. 'DROP!' he yelled desperately.

He flopped into the sand and buried his head in his hands. A great burning flame shot out from below the Messerschmitt's wings. Crooke could feel the searing heat pass over his back. He flashed a glance upwards as the second rocket came swaying towards them, gathering speed at every second, trailing fiery sparks after it. He ducked hastily. There was a loud crash and the second rocket buried itself harmlessly in the sand some fifty yards behind them.

'On your feet,' Crooke screamed as the planes roared overhead and then zoomed up into the sky again. Behind him the sand was seared a stinking black by the rocket trails. But Crooke had no time to consider their good fortune. The German pilots wouldn't give up so easily. They'd be back all right.

Then they were up and running again, the only sound that of breath coming as if it were being pumped into their bodies by a pair of ancient worn bellows. 'Zig-zag ... for hell's sake, zig-zag!' Crooke cried as the two planes completed their wide circle and lined up for their third attack.

'Taking me ... all me bloody time ... to keep running straight, sir,' Stevens panted, his face crimson with the effort.

This time the pilots, who were obviously veterans, were not going to miss. They would be hardly more than a hundred feet above the plain, their flaps and undercarriages down so that their speed was reduced appreciably. Relentlessly they came in for the kill. Behind Crooke, the Yank yelled something and came to a halt, facing the planes.

Crooke glanced over his shoulder. 'Yank,' he gasped, 'keep on running, man!'

'Screw 'em!' the Yank yelled, his chest heaving, 'I ain't running no more!'

The woods were still well over a mile away. Crooke felt his strength failing fast and stopped abruptly. One by one the others staggered to a halt and stood there on the naked plain, panting for breath, the sweat pouring down their faces. Like the helpless victims they were, they waited for the great metallic birds and their message of death.

But not the Yank. He braced himself and tried to control his breathing. Raising his Schmeisser he took careful aim at the two enemy fighters, getting closer and closer. Next to Crooke a panting Stevens pulled out the signal pistol. 'Better than nothing, sir,' he gasped. He aimed it too, ready for the moment when the Messerschmitts hit them.

Crooke felt utterly helpless, a stupid sheep waiting for the slaughter. Everything had the appearance of some ancient ritual drama, carried out according to time-honoured rules, in which the victim must inevitably die in the end.

'All right, you bastards!' the Yank shouted out. As flickers of violet flame began to run down the enemy planes' wings, he pulled the trigger of his machine pistol, standing

217

there like a duellist among the hail of lead – cool, precise, impersonal, but nothing happened.

Crooke felt the strength flee from him.

Madly the Yank fumbled with the weapon. The Me's were almost on them now. Suddenly Stevens went into action. Crouched like a western gunslinger in an old film, he fired. The brassbound pistol jerked upwards. A gout of flame shot from its bell-like muzzle. Slowly a ball of bright flame, followed by a zig-zag line of dull white smoke rose into the path of the lead plane. Suddenly it exploded. A vicious star of yellow-red burst open just in front of the pilot, blotting out all else, blinding him momentarily. Just for one fleeting second he lost control. But at that height even that was too long.

The Messerschmitt's nose dropped dangerously. It zoomed over their heads, the pilot struggling crazily for control. Suddenly it hit the ground. The wheels struck a hollow. They bounced up, and the tip of the prop splintered. There was a screech of protesting metal. The air was full of the stink of burning rubber. Then the undercarriage gave way. The Messerschmitt hit the sand with a metal-searing crash. Crazily the plane careered forward. Its nose hit a rock and crumpled like cardboard. A second later there was a tremendous explosion. The Destroyers ducked as burning wreckage hissed through the air. When it cleared there was nothing to be seen save for a burning pool of oil and a few odd bits of glowing metal.

Moments later the surviving plane was hurrying away back to sea and the dangerous belly-landing which lay in front of it. The shooting down of his companion had obviously unnerved the pilot; he had had enough.

Crooke gave the signal for them to start moving again. For a long moment the Caucasian Fox looked at the wreckage strewn over the sand in front of them, then he touched his forehead as if in salute to the dead pilot. Turning, he followed them towards the pines.

Four hours later, as the sun reached its zenith, they emerged from the trees and stared at the mountains which loomed up in front of them. Crooke held up his hand for them to halt and stared at the view.

It was rugged, tough country with here and there a path visible zig-zagging up the mountains to dizzy heights. There was little vegetation save an occasional patch of withered bent scrub. The tortured landscape was broken up otherwise only by screes and precipices. 'That's the way we've got to go,' he announced drily. 'On the other side of those mountains there's Turkey.'

'Looks like the end of the bloody world to me, sir,' Stevens said.

'All right,' Crooke said, 'Let's get our heads down for a bit. In one hour we're going to start the climb. We might as well take as much advantage of the daylight as possible. I don't want to get caught up there in the dark.'

Gippo trembled visibly. 'Must we go up there, sir?' he asked. 'I'm not liking heights. I am getting sick.'

'Don't worry, you horrible wog, you,' Stevens said sinking down to the ground with a grateful groan. 'I'll hold yer dirty little pinkie for you, never fear.'

With amused smiles, the rest of the party followed Crooke's example and retired to the shelter of the trees. Only Banu remained standing, her brown arms folded over her bosom, staring down at them.

'Sit down, miss,' Peters said and patted the scrubby grass free of pine needles for her.

She shook her head. 'I have something to

220

say,' she announced formally. She hesitated a moment, then she said, 'I am going back.'

'What!'

'Yes, there is nothing in front of you now except the mountains.'

'But you couldn't tackle that terrible journey back all by yourself,' Crooke objected, rising to his feet.

She shook her head. 'It will be easier for me. I can go straight down to the coast. Perhaps to Batumi, where I have friends. They will help me the rest of the way back to my people.'

'But what can you do there, miss?' Peters had also sprung to his feet, his face tense and worried. 'There's nothing back there for you. Come on with us to Turkey.'

'Peters is right,' Crooke agreed. 'I'm sure our people in Ankara can help you. There's nothing for you back here. Both the Russian and German authorities will undoubtedly be looking for you.'

Banu bit her lip, as if she had realised for the first time how true his words were. 'Perhaps. But you have your loyalties – and I have mine.'

Crooke shrugged and fell into silence.

'Banu,' Peters said desperately.

Her face softened a little, but her words

were hard and determined. 'I know,' she said. 'I know. But personal feelings must be set aside. I think you know that too.' She turned to the others again. 'We Circassians are political animals. The freedom of my people from the Russians is more important to me than my personal wishes.'

'I understand, Banu – and when do you want to go?'

Five minutes later they had all said their goodbyes and given her the pathetic remnants of their food – a tin of Gippo's chocolate, a piece of the tinned pumpernickel bread. 'Well, Banu,' Crooke stuck out his hand, 'there's not much more I can say – save thanks. Very many thanks.'

She took his hand and pressed it with masculine firmness. 'One day perhaps you will come back.'

'Perhaps.'

Peters, hovering by her side, said softly, 'I'll walk with you to the trees down there, miss.'

She shook her head. 'No,' she said, not looking him in the eye. 'No, that will not be necessary.'

A moment later she set off through the trees. She walked rapidly as if she wanted to get away from them. Where the path turned and disappeared into the thicker firs, they thought she might turn and wave to them. They waited expectantly. She did not even hesitate. Without looking back, Banu – 'Lady, it means in English' – went out of their lives for good.

CHAPTER EIGHT

Thirty minutes later they started their ascent. It was a long gruelling struggle. The clouds came lower as they pushed on, spread out in a long ragged file. The vegetation began to give out. The clouds became thicker. The wind swirled them around the Destroyers. Sometimes they closed in so much that they could barely see each other. Occasionally a gap opened and they could see the sandy plain a thousand or more feet below, where now Banu marched south, alone with her determination and courage.

It started to get colder. With the clouds at near freezing point and the slight wind, conditions began to get unpleasant. The first hoar frost settled on their thin clothes and whitened their beards and eyebrows so that they clambered upwards through the clouds like old, old men.

Breathing began to get difficult too. The icy cold air was too thin and after a while they were gasping for air, as if they were in the last stages of consumption. Doggedly they marched on.

The hours passed. The clouds dropped away below them. The scrub underfoot had vanished altogether now. They were approaching the snow line. Up above them the first patches, tucked away in gulleys and rock clefts, glistened brightly in the last rays of the sun. In spite of the cold their spirits picked up as they left the clouds behind them. Crooke quickened the pace, his breath fogging the crisp air. By his side the Fox, exhibiting no strain whatsoever, frowned severely. 'Mr Crooke,' he said after glancing back at the faces of the Destroyers behind him, 'I think it's about time we stopped.'

'What do you mean?' Crooke asked.

'It'll soon be dark.'

Crooke swung an impatient arm at the sun directly above them. 'It's still high in the sky.'

'Yes, but you don't know the mountains. Sixty, ninety minutes more and it'll be on the other side of that peak. Then the temperature will drop ten,' he shrugged, 'perhaps fifteen degrees in a matter of as many minutes. How do you think your men will stand up to a sudden fall like that dressed as they are?'

Crooke held up his hand for the Destroyers to stop. He could see the sense in the German's remarks. 'All right, I take your point. What do you suggest?'

'We dig ourselves in for the night and get some warm food inside of us before it gets too dark to see.'

Crooke looked at him incredulously. 'Did I hear you say warm food?'

The German nodded. 'I did indeed.'

The next hour passed quickly. While the rest scooped out a shelter in the snow, piling it up in the direction the wind was coming from, Stevens and Gippo burrowed into the rocks under the Field-Marshal's direction to look for dried moss for the fire. As he had confidently predicted, they found some and in the shelter of a rock started a poor smoky fire. 'Now start melting some snow,' he ordered, taking over with his old habit of command. 'I'll go and look for some food.'

Thirty minutes later as the sun began to pass behind the peak, he returned, his hands and pockets filled with dirty white insects.

'Our evening meal,' he said proudly, thrusting forward a sample of the wriggling mess.

'What the devil is it, sir?' Peters asked.

'Food – as I've already said.'

'Boy, if that's food,' the Yank said scornfully, 'I can use it – like I could a goddam hole in the head!'

The German explained that the insects were larvae, which thrived in the extreme heat of the mountainside in daylight, but which burrowed under the snow as soon as it began to grow cold. 'They don't look very pleasant,' he concluded. 'I admit that. But they are a very valuable source of protein. And if we are to survive a night on this mountain the way we're dressed, we need protein – plenty of it, believe you me!'

The Fox was right. The Destroyers spent the most miserable night of their lives in the little snow burrow, with the north-west wind howling over their heads. After the boiled grubs and a cup of water they fell into a deep sleep at first, exhausted by the effort of the climb. But by midnight they were shivering all over, unable to stop the chattering of their teeth, with the icy cold eating into their bones.

Some time before dawn the wind dropped and most of them fell into a restless doze, sleeping a few minutes, waking up trembling and then dropping off once more. Crooke started to pray for dawn and the sun's blessed warmth.

He was to be disappointed. When he awoke the light was still dim, hardly distinguishable from dusk, and although Crooke lay awake shivering and waiting for the sun to come up over the peak, it seemed to grow no stronger as time passed.

In the end he rose stiffly and levered himself out of the hole. Then he saw why. Up ahead the snow was coming down, not heavily but steadily in large wet flakes.

'Balls,' he cursed. Obviously the temperature had risen when the wind had dropped. Now snow was falling in a way that made it look to him as if it would go on all day. He looked at the grey, murky uninviting prospect and cursed once again.

The Fox stirred and was awake instantly. 'Snowing?' he queried.

Crooke nodded numbly.

'Thought it would – it started to get warmer about four.' He brushed a few odd flakes from his naval oilskin and clambered out of the hole. Together the two officers stared at the prospect before them.

'What do you think, sir?' Crooke asked. He no longer thought of the German as an enemy. Now they were two leaders facing up to the common danger, responsible for the safety of the men sprawled asleep in the hole at their feet.

'I don't know, Crooke,' the Field-Marshal said. His voice was calm, but he could not quite hide his anxiety. 'It's too late to go back, but I'm scared of going forward.' He spread out his hands, palms upwards in the Central European manner. 'The way we're dressed, no equipment and nothing in our bellies but a lot of maggots … I really don't know.'

Crooke said nothing, but waited anxiously, valuing the other man's superior experience in this field. The snow continued to fall in steady silence, as if it would never stop again. Still the Fox did not speak.

'My lads are tough,' Crooke volunteered. 'They've been through a lot. They can stand–'

The Field-Marshal held up his hand for silence. Grim-faced he walked to where the snow was falling. Crooke watched as he bent down and picked up a handful. He squeezed it in his fingers, opened them and regarded the snow thoughtfully. Finally he turned and walked back to Crooke.

'Crooke,' he said slowly. 'We have a saying in the German Army – *marschieren oder krepieren*.'

'Yes, I know it. "March or Die".'

229

The Field-Marshal nodded his agreement. 'Yes, march or die. Well, Mr Crooke, that is all that is left to us. With a bit of luck the snow might stop soon or turn into rain – it's very wet – but that is if God is on our side. Otherwise, it's simply march or die.'

They marched all that morning through the snow, staggering and falling time and again on the slippery slopes, their breath coming in harsh gasps, their tortured lungs threatening to burst at any moment under the strain. But the Fox, now in the lead, allowed them no respite. In spite of his own obvious exhaustion, he kept them going, cursing and cajoling them into ever greater efforts. Once Thaelmann gasped that he could not go on. The Fox left the head of the column, slipped through the snow back to where he sat on a rock, his head bowed in defeat. 'Keep moving,' he ordered over his shoulder and waved his hands at the Destroyers like a drover urging on tired cattle. He whispered something to Thaelmann in German. The Communist lifted his head slowly. 'That's it, that's it, Thaelmann,' the Fox urged him on. He grabbed hold of the other man's hand and tugged.

Reluctantly Thaelmann rose to his feet. The

officer put his arm round Thaelmann's bowed shoulders. '*Marschieren oder krepieren,*' he ordered swiftly, the force of his whole tremendous personality lending encouragement and confidence to his words. Thaelmann put one foot forward. 'Good … good, that's it!'

The Communist's other foot followed. The Fox beamed at him like a proud father watching his son make his very first steps. 'That's it, that's it, Thaelmann! Come on now, lean on me. We can't let the rest get too far ahead, can we?'

Thaelmann nodded humbly, not trusting himself to speak. The tears were streaming down his frozen cheeks unheeded, but he was moving.

Slowly the two of them moved up the slippery snow slope seemingly supporting each other. Crooke watched them come. It was a tremendous performance, one that only a great leader like the Caucasian Fox could have brought off.

The afternoon dragged on. Now it had stopped snowing and had grown colder again, but they plodded on grimly, knowing that they wouldn't survive another night on the mountainside. They had not eaten since the boiled grubs of the previous evening and their strength was failing fast. Crooke and the Fox kept them going. The peak grew closer and closer, the side of it facing Turkey still bright with the sinking sun, their side already turning a shadowy violet, indicating that sunset was not far off. Then they breasted a steep height to see a broad plain in front of them, with here and there tiny yellow lights winking up at them from the villages below.

For a moment they stood there stupidly, staring down at them, not able to take in their import. Slowly, as if he were finding it difficult to utter the words, Stevens said, 'If there are lights down there, it means we've done it.'

'Done what?' someone asked.

'We've reached Turkey. They're neutral. No blackout.'

'Turkey!' the Yank echoed after what seemed an age, swaying back and forth on the height as if he were very drunk.

Suddenly Gippo shouted '*Turkey, do you hear – TURKEY!*' There was hysteria in his eyes. Next moment their weariness vanished. They were slapping each other on the back, laughing and shouting at the tops of their voices, strained bloodshot eyes abruptly full of new life.

Thus it was that they did not see the file of short, bulky men who plodded deliberately round the spur until it was too late.

CHAPTER NINE

'*Stoi?*' the first little man challenged, levelling the business end of a tommy gun at them.

He was bulky with padded clothing, huge rucksack, from which an ice-axe stuck out, and thick mittens which hung from his neck by a ribbon. But it was not his clothing on which their eyes were fixed; it was the emblem on the front of the man's big fur hat with the earflaps tied above it. It was a simple red star with a faded gilt hammer and a sickle in its centre.

They had run into a Soviet Army border patrol!

'*Stoi?*' the little man repeated the challenge and thrust his weapon towards their stomachs threateningly, a suspicious look on his chubby, slant-eyed Mongolian face.

Crooke looked at the Fox helplessly, allowing his shoulders to sag in defeat. So close to freedom – and now this, the beat expression on his face said in abject hopelessness.

The Caucasian Fox brought up his frozen hands and then let them drop weakly, as more and more of the Red Army men gathered around them threateningly. One of them poked the Yank with his tommy gun and the American, usually so eager to take offence, tamely staggered back, his spirit broken.

Curiously, probably not quite knowing what to do with these strange ragged exhausted civilians, the Mongolians, jabbering now in their own tongue, lowered their weapons a little and began running their hands over the Destroyers tattered clothes. One of them tugged at Crooke's eye patch. It came off to reveal the raw red empty socket. He staggered back, apparently momentarily alarmed and flung a stream of words at the others. There was much nodding of heads and serious face-pulling as if the eye patch had some special significance for them.

Gippo was the first to snap out of the trance that had been induced by their disappointment. He took a step forward and crooked a finger conspiratorially at the man with the tommy gun, who had first challenged them. The man moved towards him hesitantly. Gippo tapped the black box he had salvaged from the wreck of the *Moewe* and, holding it up to his ear, rattled it loudly.

The Mongolian's eyes grew cunning. He thrust out a hand to seize it. Gippo pulled it back out of his reach quickly. The Mongolian hesitated, then dropped his hand.

Gippo nodded approvingly and smiled – a great fake Arab smile, full of promises which would never be kept. Slowly – very slowly – he opened the box, while the Mongolians crowded ever closer, full of curiosity. Deliberately Gippo pulled out the coins it contained and thrust a palmful towards them. A sigh of awe rose from their collective throats, followed a moment later by a burst of excited chatter. Gippo held up his hand for silence. The Mongolians' jabbering died away instantly.

Crooke and the rest watched bewildered, only half aware of what Gippo intended. But if they were lost, the pre-war pornography pedlar was in his element again; he was in complete charge of the situation. He had found his audience and from the look on his sharp brown face, the Destroyers could tell that Gippo thought them an audience of suckers. While their eyes rested greedily on the box, Gippo began an elaborate dumb show with his free hand. He ran his fingers along the top of a rock as if he were going for a walk. His eyes asked, did they understand?

They nodded: they understood.

He beamed his approval. He turned and swung an expansive hand at the Destroyers before making the walking gesture again. Obviously all of them were to go for a walk.

Once more the Mongolian soldiers nodded their understanding.

Gippo crooked his finger at them. He walked a few steps and made a gesture of placing the box on the ground. One of the Mongolians grabbed for it, but again Gippo beat him to it. He shook his head disapprovingly like a teacher with some naughty child, and wagged a long finger at the man who had tried to steal the box.

His big white teeth flashed the fake smile at them once more. He was their friend, perhaps their only friend in this cruel, heartless world. They nodded seriously, plainly moved by his confidence in them. Carefully, so that there would be no misunderstanding he pretended to lock the box, before miming the handing of the key to them. 'You understand?' he asked, breaking the silence for the first time, and holding up a handful of the twenty-mark gold coins, dating from the days of the old German Empire, for them to see.

Crooke doubted if they understood the half-breed's words, but they knew the money was going to be theirs all right – if they let the Destroyers go.

Then the one who had challenged them turned to his companions and said something in a quick excited tone.

A burly Mongolian with a scar running down the side of his face was doubtful. He made a gesture with his tommy gun.

'That fat bugger wants to knock us off,' Stevens whispered.

'Better pray he doesn't get his way,' Crooke said.

The unintelligible excited palaver seemed to go on forever. Down below on the plain more and more yellow lights flicked on. Night was sweeping across the villages. Gippo calmly sat down on a rock, one hand clutching the box protectively, the other trailing on the ground. Crooke wondered how he could be so damn calm when the next moment the Mongolians might simply kill them and take the money like that. But his reason told him that the catch might be that another patrol could possibly find the bodies and start asking questions back at their headquarters. If they let the Destroyers go, they could keep the money without danger.

'But would they let you go – just like that?' a grim cynical little voice within him asked. 'They might be peasant conscripts from God knows where, but they're no mugs!'

While the burly Mongolian waved his arm energetically, obviously trying to convert the others to his way of thinking, Crooke's brain raced excitedly, trying to work out the other possibilities. Then it came to him. The Mongolians would let them go. But once they were on Turkish territory – and the border could only be a matter of yards away – they'd open fire. Dead or dying they would be a Turkish problem after that and they, the Mongolians, would be able to divide up their loot and spend it without fear of discovery.

Suddenly the palaver stopped. The first Mongolian turned to them and nodded his head slowly several times as if he were addressing a bunch of thick-witted children, who needed the gesture explained to them before its meaning would penetrate into their cretinous brains. Satisfied they had understood, he held out a dirty yellow hand for the key.

Gippo rose to his feet. He was smiling again. Slowly he shook his head and went through the dumb show of walking with his fingers again.

The squat Mongolian nodded his understanding.

Without looking at them, his brown eyes fixed unwinkingly on the soldier, the smile glued to his lips, he whispered urgently, 'Go past me – quick. When I am giving them the key, you are running.'

Hastily they threaded their way through him and the suspicious Mongolians. Slowly Gippo followed, the box tucked under his arm. The Mongolians licked their thick lips greedily, their eyes fixed on it. Casually he deposited it on a rock some six feet away and made a great play of locking it.

The Mongolian who had first challenged them swallowed hard. For him the German gold coins must have represented an unbelievable fortune.

Apparently satisfied, Gippo cast a quick glance at the other Destroyers. They were already a dozen yards away. Beyond them, starkly outlined against the darkening sky, he caught sight of a large wire contraption with what looked like a portrait in its centre.

He couldn't make it out, but he could see the crescent-shaped symbol above it. The Turkish frontier!

He turned to the waiting Mongolians, the fake smile on his face. Raising the key so that they could see it, he swung it from side to side. Their beady little eyes followed it as if hypnotised. Abruptly Gippo's smile vanished. Taking a deep breath, he flung it at them. It fell at their feet in the snow. They grabbed for it, shouting excitedly.

Gippo swung round, '*RUN!*' he yelled. He did not wait for their reaction, but burst into a run. Frantically the Destroyers tumbled down the steep slope. Behind them the Mongolians fumbled excitedly with the key, trying to open the box. They were unsuccessful. The great wire contraption grew closer. The Destroyers forgot their exhaustion now. The sign was only fifty yards away.

Angrily the Mongolians tried to fit the key into the lock and turn it, but it refused to fit. In a blind rage, the burly Mongolian with the scar grabbed the box and flung it at the rock. It refused to open. He seized it again and tried to ram home the key.

The sign was only twenty yards away now. Crooke, his breath coming in gasps, recognised the face in the portrait. It was the

241

founder of the new Turkey, Kemal Ataturk, 'the Father of the Turks.' But at that moment he was not concerned with the dead dictator; his gaze was fixed on the large rocks behind the portrait which offered protection from the lead which would be coming their way at any moment.

They scrambled under the wire while from behind came the angry cries of the Mongolians. The Field-Marshal stumbled, tried to get up and sat down again with a groan. Thaelmann did not hesitate. '*Schnell!*' he urged. Thrusting his arm between the Caucasian Fox's legs, he swung the officer over his shoulders in a fireman's lift. Staggering wildly from side to side, he headed for the rocks.

A shrill cry of rage echoed down the mountainside. The Mongolians had finally discovered Gippo's trick. Even before it died away, they opened up with their tommy guns. But in their anger their aim was wild. Lead hissed through the air as the Destroyers flung themselves behind the cover of the rocks.

As they recovered their breath, heedless of the bullets still ricocheting impotently off the stones behind them, Gippo, his chest heaving, opened his skinny brown hand. In it lay a key. 'I … I gave them … the wrong one,' he panted.

Stevens patted him on the back. 'You cunning wog bugger, you!' he chortled. 'I knew you was fly, Gippo, but I didn't know you was that bloody bent!'

The rest joined in his laughter, while the half-breed, who claimed he was descended from Lord Kitchener, sat in their midst, a modest smile of achievement on his face. But he was not finished with his revelations yet. He waited till their laughter finally died away. Then he dug his hands in his pockets and pulled them out, both fists clenched. His hands were full of coins – the twenty-mark gold pieces that had been in the box!

The Yank gasped. 'Well, I'll be a sonuvabitch!' he exploded incredulously. 'How in hell's name did ya pull that one off, Gippo?' Like the rest of them he stared at the politely smiling half-breed in undis-guised awe.

'While those wog chaps was talking, I am sitting on the rock and putting stones in the box,' he said baldly, as if it were the most natural thing in the world to do and then lapsed into silence to await their reaction. It was not long coming. A great wave of laughter burst from the exhausted men crouched in the shelter of the rocks. It swept up the mountain side and echoed and re-echoed, telling the Mongolians all they needed to know. One by one they turned, shoulders slumped in defeat, and began to plod wearily through the snow deeper into their forbidding homeland.

Two hours later the Destroyers staggered into Kars. In the gloom they could make out a deep gorge to one side with a fortress poised above it, a red-roofed mosque and the usual rickety wooden Turkish houses lining the wide dusty streets.

From all sides the lean moustached Turks crowded in to watch their stumbling drunken progress down the streets. A couple of shabby policemen, wearing what looked like World War One British helmets, tried to stop them. The Destroyers pushed them to one side without ceremony. The policemen joined the rest of the crowd following these strange ragged men who had appeared from nowhere. Stevens took the lead, sniffing the warm night air, heavy with the spicy smell of Turkish cooking, following his nose like some two-legged hunting dog. Then he found what he was looking for – a shabby open-air restaurant, flares hissing among the stained tables. A waiter barred their way, his weak face strengthened by a huge 'Kaiser Bill' moustache. Stevens brushed by him, nostrils twitching as he smelt the odour of cooking which came from the dirty open kitchen at the end of the restaurant.

Behind him Gippo yelled at the waiter, '*Bira – bira lutfen.*' He took a handful of coins out of his pocket and threw them carelessly on the nearest table.

The waiter's eyes bulged. Hurriedly, he grabbed them before they could roll away. '*Bira,*' he yelled frantically at the skinny tousled boy who had appeared at the door of the kitchen, wiping the sweat off his brow with a tea-cloth. '*Bira!*'

Suddenly the restaurant was full of excited noise. Someone switched on the public address system. The night was broken by the thin tortured wail of Turkish music. Big litre bottles of beer were put down on their table by a suddenly beaming waiter, foam spurting everywhere.

'*Cok gusel,*' the circle of awe-stricken ragged Turks gasped as the food began to arrive – plate after plate of it. Steaming kebabs, piles of lamb chops, salads of aubergines, cucumbers and sour cream, stewed chickens. More and more disappeared effortlessly into the stomachs of the starved men to the cries of '*cok gusel.*'

And as the raki, the milky white Turkish schnapps, flowed in streams, the first messages started to go out from the little forgotten border town. From the police HQ at the provincial capital they reached the Turkish Ministry of the Interior. Hurriedly the humble little clerk in the Minister's outer office excused himself after he had read the flimsy. Half an hour later he was standing in the office of the British Military Attaché at the Embassy. Money changed hands swiftly. Sixty minutes later the encoded message was on its way to the MI6 representative in the old part of Istanbul.

The MI6 man dropped his plans to go to a party where he hoped to contact new defectors from Major Leverkuehn's local branch of the German *Abwehr*. He wasted no time. He radioed the news personally to his HQ in Cairo.

Cairo recognised its urgency at once. The unit's radio operator was roused out of his bed in spite of the lateness of the hour. Grumbling and scratching his head in bewilderment, he waited till the unit's head encoded the message in the new top-secret MI6 code. Within thirty minutes it was on its way to England.

Five hours later just as the night shift at the great Secret Intelligence wireless station at Bletchley Park, some thirty miles north-west of the capital, was starting to wonder when their relief operators would make an appearance, it began to come in. Decoding took a matter of minutes. The wires to London began to hum. To the office of the Directorate of Naval Intelligence in Whitehall, the MI6 branches in Queen Anne's Gate and Ealing, Philby's Section V at Prae Wood, Number Ten Downing Street with the cover slip 'For Your Eyes Only.'

Telephones rang. Dispatch riders ran to their machines. Top priority telegrams were rushed to the provinces. Excited night duty officers, unable to reach their superiors in any other way, rushed across London by taxi to wake them personally. For the news that was coming in from Bletchley Park was tremendous. 'DESTROYERS REPORTED BACK ... ON TURKISH BORDER ... MISSION THOUGHT SUCCESSFUL ... RELIABLY REPORTED ... CAUCASIAN FOX IN BRITISH HANDS.'

SECTION FOUR:
DEATH COMES TO THE
CAUCASIAN FOX

'The way things are going to develop, Crooke, the Destroyers – and anyone else who is prepared to fight fire with fire – are our only hope.'

Commander Mallory to Lt. Crooke, 1943

'Willya just get a load of that,' the Yank said scornfully, gesturing at the brass, British and German, who were beginning to fill up the drab lecture hall of Wilton Park POW camp.

'Yer,' Stevens whispered, 'if it moves, salute it. If it doesn't, pick it up – and if you can't pick it up, paint it!'

The other Destroyers laughed dutifully at the old Army litany. Commander Mallory lit yet another cigarette and looked at Crooke. He shook his head sadly and said, 'What a bunch of rogues you Destroyers are! Is nothing sacred to them?'

Crooke grinned. 'I don't know about that, but I do know I've never seen so many brasshats on one spot since the Coronation. Where the devil did they dig them all up from?'

'I don't know too much about digging them up. Some of them have come a long way for this meeting. The big fellow – the Brigadier – with the dark hair, can you see?'

'Yes.'

'That's Strong, Eisenhower's chief-of-

251

intelligence. He was assistant military attaché in Berlin before the war. He's come all the way from North Africa for this. And the chap next to him – the American colonel – that's Colonel Bruce, head of the London branch of the OSS. All the big cheeses are here, as you can see.'

Crooke followed the direction of his gaze and saw C, now dressed in the uniform of a major-general, his thin chest decorated with the MC and DSO. 'So I see.'

'Yes, our dear friend even abandoned White's for this.'

Crooke glanced around at the senior German officers present. Most of them he could not recognise, but there were several faces in the front row that he knew had featured prominently in the front pages of the British papers in these last months – von Arnim, von Thoma, Cruewell and Rommel's former second-in-command before he had been captured with the rest in North Africa *General der Panzertruppe:* Kurt Meyer.

'Panzermeyer' as the Africa Corps had nicknamed him, sitting in his black tank uniform, studiously avoided the looks of the British generals on the platform, his big arms crossed over his barrel chest in trained military patience. Unlike the rest of his high-ranking comrades, who were obviously wondering why they had been brought from their camps all over England for this sudden meeting, he was silent and self-assured, almost suspiciously so.

'Let's hope the Caucasian Fox pulls it off,' Crooke said. Mallory stubbed out one cigarette and immediately lit another. 'Let us just. The PM's put enough work into arranging all this. As you can imagine there were those in the cabinet, especially from the old Opposition, who didn't like the idea one bit. But you know what the Old Man's like once he gets the bit between his teeth – nothing can stop him.'

Crooke smiled. 'You're right enough there.' He remembered the Caucasian Fox's first meeting with the British Prime Minister two weeks before when they had been rushed from the Istanbul plane as soon as it landed at Croydon and driven at a terrifying speed through the back lanes to the great man's country residence at Chequers.

Churchill had received them in his bath, his false teeth in a glass on its edge, a big cigar in one hand and a tumbler of brandy in the other, as if it were the most natural thing in the world to welcome guests in this manner.

The Prime Minister had waved them to make themselves at ease the best they could, and while the Destroyers crowded around the door, he said in his throaty voice: 'I am glad to see you in this country, Field-Marshal, though I am no doubt certain you would like to be elsewhere.'

Surprisingly enough the Fox had not jumped at the bait. 'Perhaps, sir,' he answered carefully, 'it is better that I am here now.'

'You mean that because the Gestapo are becoming aware that you are a member of the group of generals who are planning to assassinate that man?' the Prime Minister had asked.

'How did you know, sir, about our plan to get rid of the Führer?'

Churchill, pleased with the effect of his words, had laughed throatily. Wagging his cigar at the Field-Marshal, he said: 'Ah, my dear Field-Marshal, I am afraid that your people tend to talk too much. Less talk and more action and we might both have not been in the mess that we are in today. Our Intelligence people have known about the plot to kill your Austrian corporal since 1942.'

'I see, sir. But you must not underestimate us altogether. It is true we have hesitated a lot in the past. But after Stalingrad and this new defeat in Russia at Kursk, I think my comrades will now be forced to take action – real action.'

Churchill had held up his cigar to stop him like a policeman at a traffic crossing holding up a baton. 'One minute, we shall discuss that in a moment.' He turned to the Destroyers crowded in the door, watching the amazing little scene with wide eyes. 'Let me say goodbye to these rogues here first. Crooke, you've done a good job of work. You and your men have my thanks. But that is about all you will get I am afraid. 'Brooke has told me there will be no decorations in this for you, never mind promotion.' He had looked at them keenly for one long moment and then dismissed them with, 'As far as the Regular Army goes, the Destroyers are beyond the pale – they simply do not exist.'

Their reception by C at Queen Anne's Gate later that day had seemed to confirm the PM's gloomy statement. He listened with unconcealed impatience to Crooke's account of their mission. Then he had said irritably. 'Very well then, so you have pulled it off again. I hope our Russian friends are appreciative of your efforts. I can't say that I am.' He had turned to Mallory sitting silently in the background. 'I presume you saw *The Times* this morning. Great Russian victory at Kursk. What utter rot!'

Crooke had flushed angrily, but he was not afraid of this old frail man who had so much power in his hands. 'There is another matter I'd like to mention, sir,' he had said aggressively.

'Go on then.'

'It's this business with our reception committee which wasn't there. The fact that Loladze must have known who we were, yet he wanted to kill us. Then there are the ten cases of British stens. Where did they come from?' He had stared accusingly at the head of the Secret Intelligence Service. 'To say the least, Mr Philby of your organization seems to have been badly misinformed about the situation in the Caucasus.'

C had stared at him coldly with his pale blue eyes. 'I don't like you, Crooke, nor your command. I'll be frank about that. I would be only too happy if I could do without your kind. Unfortunately I can't. You are too useful and we still have need of you. But let me say this, if it ever came to a decision between you and Kim Philby, then I would decide on Mr Philby – and you and your thugs could go back where you belong –

into jail!' And with that he had dismissed them with a contemptuous wave of his thin hand.

Twenty years later the knowledge of Philby's treachery would break his heart and hurry him to his death by his own hand; but that time was a long way off.

Outside the Destroyers had protested angrily to Mallory, but the urbane old Etonian had waved them to silence. 'It's no use going on at me like that,' he had said. 'Philby is obviously the old man's blue-eyed boy and there's nothing you can do about it. Once C gets an idea in his head, nothing can drive it out.'

'What about a stick of dynamite?' The Yank had suggested.

Mallory had wagged a finger at him. 'Naughty, naughty! You can't make statements about the head of the British Intelligence Service like that.'

'Where's Philby now?' Crooke had asked.

'Somewhere far from here where you can't – er – have a little discussion with him,' Mallory said hastily, knowing full well what Crooke's intention was. 'In the Med – Portugal, I think – working on a new op the SIS have just got going there.'

And with that the frustrated Destroyers

had been forced to drop the Philby matter. The process of forgetting had been helped by an extended leave, which had been interrupted at the Destroyers' own request so that they could attend this address by the Field-Marshal, which was the culmination of the German's several meetings with the British Prime Minister.

There was a sudden hush in the drab hall. Two armed MP majors ushered in the Caucasian Fox. In the milder English climate his colour was beginning to fade, but his old style had not changed since the Destroyers had last seen him. His step was firm and confident and unlike his fellow German prisoners, he was wearing a simple uniform, devoid of badges of rank or the decorations which adorned the chests of the others. Hastily Brigadier Kenneth Strong, Eisenhower's Chief-of-Intelligence, rose, indicated that the Field-Marshal should take a seat while he went to the rostrum. '*Meine Herren,*' he said in German.

The soft hum of chatter died away immediately, but the prisoners' eyes were not fixed on the brigadier, but on the man sitting behind him. '*Ich brauche Ihnen den Generalfeldmarschall nicht vorzustellen. Sie kennen ihn ja alle von fruher...*' In his fluent

German he introduced the Field-Marshal, then indicated that the rostrum was free. Slowly the Caucasian Fox rose to his feet and walked to the rostrum.

For a long moment he did not speak. He swung his head slowly from side to side, as if he were trying to imprint each individual face upon his memory; as if he were also searching for something that lay behind their curious eyes.

Then he began to speak in a firm, precise voice, while Thaelmann sitting at the back of the hall with the other Destroyers gave them a whispered rapid translation.

'Comrades, I am sorry to see you here again in this place after so many years. But in a way I am glad. Why?' He answered his own question. 'Because here you are free.'

There were a few snickers from the hall. In the front row Panzermeyer grinned scornfully, but still he did not move from his rigid position. 'You laugh, but it is true. Here we are at last free to do something which it would be impossible to do in our native country.' He hesitated a moment. 'I know our whole training goes against it. After all most of us have served our Fatherland loyally for over thirty years. All the same we have to take this action and you all know it.

You, von Thoma, you, von Arnim – you know it as well as I do.'

The two senior generals lowered their eyes as if they were ashamed.

'In Germany there will be some who will now try a more violent course.'

'He obviously means the murder of Hitler,' Thaelmann explained.

'Here we must attempt something else to back up those brave men and women who not only have to face their conscience like we do, but also physical danger at the hands of the Gestapo. Shall we otherwise sit out the war here, getting fat in the bottom, playing chess, learning English – improving our minds, risking nothing while our poor country bleeds to death? Or shall we do something, comrades?'

'What do you suggest?' Panzermeyer asked.

The Caucasian Fox looked at the black-uniformed Panzer leader, his breast covered with decorations. 'Thank you for the question, Meyer,' he said gravely. He addressed the assembly again. 'You all know that the Russians have formed a new committee of captured German officers under General von Seydlitz. We know the Russians' intentions. Let us not be mistaken about them.

They are no friends of the German officers corps. They will use the unfortunate von Seydlitz and then drop him when he is no longer needed.'

He paused and let his words sink in. There was absolute silence in the hall. The two MP officers, who obviously understood German, had taken their hands off their revolvers now and were listening to the Caucasian Fox completely absorbed in this talk.

'Comrades, we too, must organise ourselves! We must take an active part in this war again! We must help to bring the rule of that criminal in Berlin to an end before our country is overrun by the Reds! We must act *now!*' He rapped out the sentences in short harsh gasps, emphasising each point by hammering on the desk before him with his clenched fist.

'How?' Panzermeyer asked coldly, completely unimpressed, his little tight mouth opening and closing quickly like a rat trap.

The Caucasian Fox licked his lips. *'Mein lieber Meyer,'* he began, 'by doing exactly what von Seydlitz has done – form a committee of officers who will work with the Western Allies to put an end to this dreadful war.'

'But what of our oath of loyalty to the

Führer?' von Thoma asked in an outraged voice. 'Our honour as German officers?' There was a ripple of shocked protest through the hall. The Caucasian Fox raised his hands to stop it. *We must!* he yelled. 'Even if it does go against the code of conduct of a German officer. The days of false pride are over. These are desperate times and desperate measures are needed. Our personal vanity is of little importance in this time of Germany's greatest need.' He did not wait for them to object again. Now he was every inch the Field-Marshal, used to giving commands without question. 'I have prepared a list of names of those of you who I think could be well represented on our committee – the Free German Officers of Great Britain.'

As he fumbled with the piece of paper he had taken from his pocket, Panzermeyer rose slowly from his seat, his arms still folded across his barrel chest. Casually he strolled to the rostrum while the British officers seated there stared at him in bewilderment. 'Am I a member of your committee?' he asked coming level with the Caucasian Fox.

The Fox looked up. 'Yes, Meyer, in spite of your—' his words ended suddenly in a harsh cry of agony.

'*Verrater-verdammter Verrater!*' Meyer bellowed.

The Field-Marshal's face contorted with pain as Meyer stuck the knife into his belly once more, grunting savagely. For one long moment no one seemed able to move. Meyer thrust his knife home again. Then all was chaotic uproar. A cry of horror rose from the hall. Chairs were overturned. Someone cried in German 'Stop him!' One of the MP officers blew a whistle. The doors were flung open to reveal hard-raced red-caps armed with sten guns.

'Come on,' Crooke yelled.

Followed by Thaelmann and Mallory, he clawed and pushed his way through the confused mass of high-ranking German officers. On the platform the Field-Marshal lay on the floor, his big hands clasped to his stomach, his face deathly white. Blood was seeping through his tightly clasped fingers.

Around him the senior British officers had formed a horrified semicircle, but they did not dare move closer. Meyer, his chest heaving as if he had just run a race, crouched there, his blood-stained knife held at the ready.

'You swine – you murderous swine!'

Thaelmann shouted at him.

Meyer did not seem to hear; his eyes were fixed on the dying Field-Marshal with almost hypnotic fascination.

Thaelmann bent down and rested the Fox's head on his knees. All was silent save for Meyer's harsh breathing. No one moved. The Field-Marshal's eye flickered open for a moment. 'It's you, Thaelmann,' he said weakly, his broad face suddenly thin and pinched.

'Yes, but don't talk, Field-Marshal,' the German communist whispered, tears starting up in his brown eyes.

'Stupid,' he fought for breath, 'stupid way … to die, Thaelmann … yes?' His big blond head fell to one side. The Caucasian Fox was dead.

Gently Thaelmann lowered the Field-Marshal's body to the floor. But he did not move. He remained bent on one knee, as if deep in prayer.

Suddenly Crooke brought his fist down hard on Meyer's hand. The blood-stained knife clattered to the floor, and his dazed look vanished, to be replaced by a look of fear.

He backed away. Like a trapped animal, his eyes darted from right to left, looking for a way of escape. The Destroyers began to crowd in on him. Panzermeyer moved. A big MP major tried to stop him. Meyer kneed him brutally. The Major sank to his knees, his scream strangled by the sudden vomit. Before anyone could stop him, Meyer had dragged the man's pistol out, yanking the lanyard from around the major's neck. 'Get back,' he cried desperately, as the Destroyers moved closer, 'get back or I'll shoot!'

The Destroyers came on.

Meyer's eyes filled with absolute fear at the icy-cold looks on their killers' faces. He cocked the trigger. 'I'll shoot,' he quavered '...I promise you, if you don't get back–'

He never finished his threat. Suddenly Peters dived forward in a low tackle. Meyer was caught by surprise. He fell heavily, the bullet winging its way into the wooden rafters harmlessly. Then the Destroyers fell upon him and the slaughter of the German killer began.

Horrified, the British general officers tried to stop them. 'I order you to cease at once!' S snapped in his thin voice. 'For God's sake, can't anyone stop the crazy nuts!' Colonel Bruce of the OSS yelled desperately, as the Destroyers' fists and boots thudded in to the defenceless bleeding wreck at their feet.

'*Crooke, my God, this is a massacre – cold-blooded murder.*' C yelled. '*Make them stop – at once.*'

Crooke did not react. He watched the murder with icy control, his arms folded across his chest.

Finally it was all over. The redcaps burst through the throng of German officers and pulled them away, bundling them to one side to reveal the bloody mess of what had once been *General der Panzertruppe* Meyer. The killer of the Caucasian Fox was an almost unrecognisable corpse.

Wearily Crooke and Mallory walked around the drab compound, inhabited by a few shuffling POWs in dyed battledress. A thin rain had started to fall, but they did not notice it. 'What will happen to the Destroyers?' Crooke asked tonelessly.

Mallory took his eyes off two prisoners, squatting in the rain trying to poke some insect into a pool with a twig. 'They'll have to stay in the cooler for a couple of days. C insisted on that.' He shrugged. 'But they'll be let out again, never fear. C knows he needs your chaps.' He lapsed into silence once more.

Ahead of them the big gate swung open to

266

admit the staff car which had been sent to pick them up after their original vehicle had been commandeered to take the Destroyers away to the nearest military prison. They had gone tamely, their faces deathly pale, utterly drained of emotion by the death of the Caucasian Fox. Only Stevens, his hat gone and a thin streak of blood down the side of his face, had managed to find words as one of the big, hard-faced redcaps had shoved him into the vehicle. 'He was a good 'un, sir – a real good 'un!' he had said, tears in his eyes.

Mallory watched the big Humber staff car bump its way through the puddles. 'The car,' he said.

'What a mess – what a bloody mess,' Crooke said. 'Where will we ever find another German like the Fox?'

Mallory nodded glumly, as the car came to a halt and the driver stepped out to open the door for them. Standing there impatiently, the rain dropping on his white naval cap, his face seemed to ask why the hell they were hanging around so long in this miserable dump!

Mallory caught the look and straightened his shoulders. He put his hand on Crooke's bowed shoulder and steered him gently

267

towards the waiting car. 'Come on, Crooke, let's get out of the rain. It's no good our getting pneumonia. Operation Caucasian Fox is over – it's history now.'

They got into the car. Hastily the naval rating closed the door behind and thrust the big Humber into first, as if he couldn't get out of the camp soon enough. In low gear, it splashed through the puddles, its wipers flashing back and forth noisily as they tried to wipe away the great glutinous tears of rain which flung themselves at the sloping windscreen. Mechanically the two officers acknowledged the salutes of the steel-helmeted, middle-aged sentries.

The rating changed up. The Humber gained speed. Desperately Mallory tried to shake himself out of his mood of black despair. 'Crooke,' he said suddenly, 'this war is going to end in chaos.'

Crooked nodded numbly in agreement. He did not speak.

'It's going to end,' Mallory fumbled for words. 'Not with a whimper like in November 1918 – but with a bang, one great awful bloody rotten bang!'

'And the Destroyers?' Crooke broke his silence. 'What of my men now?' Mallory did not reply immediately. The driver had slowed down again. They were passing through the high street of one of the shabby suburbs. Outside a bare-windowed butcher's, shabby housewives in curlers and headscarves were standing in a long patient queue by a sign on which was scrawled in white paint: 'LIVER TODAY! FOR RATION BOOKS A TO H.'

As the car passed, the women huddled together against the rain, did not look up. Mallory shuddered. Suddenly with the uncanny awareness of a vision he knew that the scene typified his – everybody's – post-war world. 'The Destroyers?' he echoed hollowly. 'The way things are going to develop, Crooke, the Destroyers – and anyone else who is prepared to fight fire with fire – are our only hope.'

The Humber splashed on through the dirty puddles of a wartime afternoon into the grey harsh barren world to come.